CONFLICTED

Billie Dureyea Shell

CONFLICTED

Copyright © 2022

All rights reserved to Billie Dureyea Shell.

No part of this publication may be reproduced, distributed or transmitted in any form or by any means, including photocopying, or other electronic or mechanical methods, without the prior written permission of the publisher, except in the case of brief quotations embodied in critical reviews and certain noncommercial uses permitted by copyright law. Any references to historical events, real people or real places are used factiously. Names, characters, and places are products of the authors imagination.

Front Cover Image by graphic designer
Billie Dureyea Shell & Kenny Writes

First Printing Edition 2022

ISBN: 978-1-7373922-9-3

A Not to All My Readers and Fans

What's up y'all I decided to dedicate this book to all the people that ever had a dream and someone tried to steal their Joy. Here's food for thought a mother fucker without a dream will always try to kill yours facts and know this the hate won't always come from outside your circle sometimes, shit A lot of the times it's motherfuckers that smile in your face that's behind you back talking about you 80% of the hate thats thrown at you will be from people you know or that you thought you was cool with don't waste your time trying to be cool with people who cares about what people think haters are breeding just like dogs what I mean by that is this just like a dog or should I say a puppy you can tell what kind of person someone is going to be by their parents so more than likely if someone's a hater they come from a long line of haters there mama and their daddy was haters their grandma and their grandpa was haters so it's in their

DNA it was inevitable that they was going to be a hater so let there hate motivate you to be greater haters going to hate it ain't nothing that you can do about it let them do what they do and you continue to do what you do and Shine. I mean who gives a fuck if they don't like you you can't expect everybody to have good taste I'm out don't forget to leave a comment about the book at Barnes and Nobles Amazon or anywhere you buy the book at I love y'all keep your heads up

Author
Billie Dureyea Shell

Acknowledgement

What's up y'all first and foremost I want to thank all my readers for buying the books that I've been putting out and supporting this journey that I'm going on writing. You guys have really made this writing shit something that I love to do the more you read it the more I write it without y'all putting these books out wouldn't even be worth it so I thank y'all and I love you all 2022 is here so let's get it......... To my Lord and Savior Jesus Christ thank you for blessing me with this talent and these skills I love you more than words could ever say you died on the cross for me and I know I wasn't worthy of it, so every day I'm going to try to prove to you that it wasn't in vain. To my mother, Mom I love you more than words could ever say we've been through the storm in the rain and we still here he was the first woman to ever have my back and I will always love you for that you know there's nothing that I won't do for you. And there's not enough money in the world to pay you back for all the shit I sent you through but I hope it was the things I am doing for you now I'm showing you how much you will appreciate it you always be my number one girl I love you Mama. To my little sister Glenda I miss you and I love you, you know I got your back no matter what and no matter what we go through I got to never change. To my beautiful wife and the love of my life Shatoya I never thought and I could find somebody that I would love just as much as I love myself yet a lot more everything that I have is yours and my heart belongs to you you always tell me that I'm the best part of you or little do you know you're the best part of me you get on my nerves and sometime I wonder is that your job. I love you for now forever and for always 1437. Call my kids and it's a lot of y'all so let's start in age order:

Jazmine, Ant'Juan, Devon, David, little Dureyea, Dillon, Alura, Avi, Cameron, Premiere, Shanice, and Anthony I love all of y'all you guys are the reason I smile. To my grandchildren Jordan, little Devon, and little Roman I love each one of y'all to Uncle Woody thank you for all you done in helping me to become a man you will always be my favorite uncle and a person I turned to for advice when this world get too hectic for me. To my cousin Zane R.I.P nigga I miss you more than words could ever express but just know that I'm down here holding it down and taking care of business and I promise you you'll never be forgotten. Call my nieces and nephews I love you all. To my big brother Lawrence thank you for all that you've done for me and showing me how to get it to my even older brother Fred you maybe you crazy but I still love you to my little cousin

Cella you know I got you when you need me and I love you we are the fuck we got and we all fuck we need. To My uncle Woody only son R.I.P you messed and we love you and you won't be forgotten. To everybody else I didn't mention it ain't that I forgot you you just you just wasn't worth mentioning to all my dark side niggas you already know what it is keep doing what you're doing. Oh yeah a few shots cuz I don't want these people to think I'm saying fuck them Margo love you little sister Sade Love You Selena love you Shay Shay love you little Brandon and Lil Brian love y'all auntie Chris love you shit I think that's about it now enough of all this mushy stuff let's get to this book I hope you all enjoy reading as much as I enjoyed writing Happy New Year it's 2022 stay safe keep your mess on and let's get this money .....

Author Billie Dureyea Shell

Chapter 1

Sitting upright and confident in a park chair opposite a wooden chess board, Detective Sensi Mendez faced his amateur opponent wearing a self-assured, smug grin. He sat comfortably under a lamp-post near a large oak tree at the far side of the Hackney Downs Community Park in East London, which gave him a complete view of the bustling high street ahead whilst he was hidden by the trees branches and autumn coloured leaves. "You planning on telling me what›s on your mind, or you gonna stay eyeballing the board to catch my move?» The detective's young and undefeated challenger asked, seeing the detective's impatience while he studied the board to make a move. He took his eyes off the board for a brief moment before finally administrating his move. "Play, son." The Detective said, looking up at his opponent and gesturing for him to make a move. He then pulled a cigar out the inside pocket of his trench coat, and popped it into his mouth letting it droop slightly. "Don't worry about me old man, I got this," the young man replied as he leaned back in his chair full of attitude. He gave Sensi his undivided attention and waited patiently for what the detective had to say. "What makes you think I called you for anything else other than a friendly game? You know I very rarely like to mix business with our time." Sensi said stealing a move within the blink of his opponent's eyes. 'Our time?" His opponent turned up his nose at the thought. 'This nigga wants something, I can tell.' "Because I know you, you play dirty even when you're playing against your own, but it's all good." The young man said studying the board. "This is my game, and there ain't anything you can do to throw me off it. I'm about to take your knight out." He laughed out loud and pointed at the playing board. Sensi had arranged what was left of his playing pieces till they were scattered across the board, though there was a single knight protecting two pawns and a bishop. "You need to stop protecting these little nigga's and stay focused on your queen, cause if she gets knocked... its game over." The young man continued whilst anticipating his next move. "In chess, yes, you're correct." Sensi said. "But out here you're so wrong." He chimed before lighting his cigar and exhaling the smoke in the opposite direction. "It's like this, try to think of your queen as your woman or, how do you youngster's say it? You're wifey or boo." The middle-aged detective laughed, mocking the words the youngsters used in the streets today. "Naturally you're the King and the board is your domain." He coughed, and took his time catching his breath before he wheezed on. "Most of you youngen's spend your time chasing one bitch." He cackled, then spat on the ground. "Now that I think about it, you're all out here chasing the same bitch." He coughed again, spitting out some saliva while wiping his mouth with the end of his hand then motioning to his opponent to make his move. Detective Sensi and his opponent, Essen Boaten, comically bantered over their futile c'hess game, the rules of the streets, and the lifestyle they often called 'the game.' Both men played exceptionally well, but it was neither to win nor lose. They played to strategize their position in the game, playing out their lives on the board. "See, there you go getting me mixed up with your son. I know for a fact you ain›t tryna put me in that category. When have you ever seen me chasing a bitch? Let alone a bitch some other pricks' claiming," Essen snapped. He shook his head, and moved his bishop taking one of the detective's pawns out of the game. "Power is your bitch, Essen." The detective said raising his voice. "Power and respect, and that skirt you and Judas are chasing is the lifestyle that comes with her. I've seen so many little nigga's in my time, just like you and Judas, trying to juggle them all and fail. Like two out of the three ain't enough. But that's why I put you down young man, because nobody smells your bitch. I see her, but I ain't smelt her yet." Sensi said puffing once and coughing twice. He laughed. "Take a good look at the board son, your queen is defenseless without you, yet she is the alpha and omega of the game. You own her world yet you're at her command. Show a bit of love to your other players once in a while, and they got just as much to lose as you do, if not more." "You're going mental Mr. M." Essen laughed. "Power and respect," He repeatedly mocked whilst studying the board for his next move in the game. Sensi shifted in his seat uncomfortably whilst Essen laughed his old school theories off, but deep down he knew Essen would heed his words. He had known Essen since the late 70s. Back when Essen was a little ashy kneed boy, now sitting before him a man. A worthy opponent if he had to choose one. Essen had long showed his loyalty and devotion to the detective, unlike his own son Judas. The two men were the complete opposite, yet they would die for each other if they were given the chance. Essen was humble, well-educated and level headed whilst Judas's arrogance and attractive looks prevailed over all other abilities in his line of work. Judas was ineffective when it came to following direct orders; therefore making any type of decisions on his own regarding the team was forbidden. Sensi had to resort to manipulation to get his 34-year-old son to adhere to the significant role the detective had fought so hard for him to obtain. "Fuck all that Mr. M! I got your power and respect right here!" said Essen seriously, as he lifted up the bottom of his t-shirt for the detective to glance at the 9 mm handgun tucked between his jeans, and pressed up securely against his waist. "And you don't ever have to worry about your people smelling me either." He brushed his hand against the steel, covering it back up before turning his attention back to the table as Sensi made his move. People in Hackney sang Essen's praises like Brooklyn did Jay-Z's, except Essen was much darker in complexion and of Nigerian decent. At age 35, Essen owned properties in Lagos, Nigeria, a town house in LA and a £259,000 penthouse apartment in London where he currently laid his head. Essen was always neat and clean shaven, and dressed from head to toe in black. Yet, he never drowned himself in the latest designer clothes or jewels as Judas did. However, whether 'all blingged out' or not, the females in the hood stayed on his dick 24/7. While Essen wasn't as flashy with his things, he still had swag; it's just his priorities laid elsewhere. As the young victim of a village fire that stole his parents' and younger brother, Essen had come to England as a child, craving the love and compassion that was stolen from him when his family died. He stayed true to his roots and educated himself on his Nigerian heritage and culture, proudly wearing it on his sleeve. No woman had ever come close to replacing the love that he'd once had as a child, or filling the void that had long taken residence in his heart. "Now we're playing chess." Essen said rubbing his hands together over the board. He sat up straight in his seat, and a rush of excitement rushed through him as he watched the detective take out the same bishop who had taken out his pawn. "You should be careful who you send out to do your bidding Essen. Was it worth risking an important player so early in the game?" Sensi asked. He saw that he had his opponent's queen covered, and attempted to call his bluff. "Well ain't this a bitch." Essen muttered whilst his eyes darted over the board. "You got me backed up yeah, I'll admit that, but I ain't ready to pack it up yet. You got me seriously twisted if you think I'm about to cry over a fuckin bishop when I got so many players left in the game." Essen screwed up his face in concentration. "In about two minutes, I'm gonna steel your knight who you've been neglecting, leaving you with no option but to protect your own damn bitch. And before you can even think of a plan to attack, my baby will have moved and I'll be one step closer to tapping your girl's ass." Essen said doubled over in laughter.

"But you lost three." Sensi said sternly, no longer concerned with the playing pieces on the board. "What you talking about?" Essen composed himself meeting eyes with the detective, forgetting about the game. "You lost three men today damnit," Sensi growled pounding the playing table with his fist causing the pieces to topple over and out of place on the board. 'I knew this nigga had something up his ass,' Essen thought, as he looked up calmly at the Detective. "Again we find ourselves in an uncomfortable place, a place where we both have to step out of our comfort zones to put right what the people around us have done wrong. I know I've already asked much of you Essen but this is something I cannot administrate on my own." The detective said as he stood up, removing himself from the game. "Walk with me to my car." Sensi commanded over his shoulder, slowly walking to the entrance of the park where he had parked his car by the pavement on the side of the road. Essen slowly removed himself from the playing table and caught up with him, and together they both walked through the dimly lit park in silence until they had reached their parked cars. "Your bishops can't be trusted," the detective said firmly, unlocking his car door. "I already have a confession of breaking an entry along with an attempted robbery on tape from two of your guys, and the others can only remain silent for so long." "Where did you find these little cunts?" the detective demanded, looking back at Essen. "You're asking the wrong man." Essen held up his hands, "You know I don't fuck with outsiders. Judas does the recruiting when it comes to the team, and I've been laying low after that shit you put me down on a couple of months back. All I know is there're a couple of knuckle-heads from down south trying to put in some work to make a little dough." "Best thing for you to do is to send 'em home with a warning or drop 'em a little thinking time." He suggested, hoping the old man would show some heart and spare the kid's hard time. "Nah, it's just too big of a risk Essen, the Superintendent can't find out about this operation. I won't let some south slanging hoodlums ruin my reputation; not now that I've brought us this far," Sensi responded raising his voice as he got into his black, tinted M3 BMW, and buckled up. "I said I got you Mr. M." Essen stressed patting his tool through his shirt. He leaned back on the park railings and tried to convince the Detective to calm down. "They're just a bunch of kids, they don't have anything on me or Judas, and they sure as hell haven't got shit on you," he calmly said. "No, we need to deal with this and see it through." Sensi said almost paranoid as he revved up the engine. He shut his door and rolled down the window. "I really appreciate what you did for me Essen. I know I don't need to ask if you read what was in that file you tracked down for me." "Say no more Mr. M". Essen replied understanding his old friend well. Three months ago the Detective had him track down a private investigator that had been employed to do some digging. He'd pulled up some files dirty enough to not only denounce the Detective's name and end his career, but also land him in jail. Sensi had a fair amount of skeletons in his closet but it was nothing that Essen could judge him on. "Same time next week yeah?" Essen suggested, referring to his and the Detective's weekly chess game in the park. "Of course Essen, I'll be in touch, but I don't wanna smell you until then." Sensi laughed as he pulled another cigar out his inside pocket and balanced it in his mouth before putting his foot down and speeding off into the darkness of the night.

Chapter 2

"Is there something I can assist you ladies with?" asked a young, pale skinned store clerk who stood posted at the front desk. She cleared her throat in order to attract the attention of the three ladies who had entered the elegant boutique in Hampstead Heath. The ladies paid the clerk, along with a middle aged white couple who seemed to be having some kind of relationship break down in the far end of the store, little to no-mind. Instead, they greeted the small, stocky, security guard who stood at the entrance with a smile, then separated throughout the store slipping cautiously into their positions. "Umm, Ladies, can I help you?" asked the store clerk once again, whose name tag read 'Ginger.' She approached them all, but was clearly speaking to Brittany. "No, no thank you. Not right now." Brittany politely responded stunning the girl with her smile. Her olive tanned completion and jet black hair always gave her a lot of attention, but not even her blue eyes could out shine the gold-plated tooth she'd had set in when she was seventeen. Slightly intimidated the store clerk backed off but kept her eyes glued on the breathtaking image of the woman before her. Every Saturday for the past eight months, Ginger assisted Brittany while she visited Pandora, just watching as she did her thing. The store clerks in Hampstead Heath paid little attention to their wealthy customers and had proved to be exceptionally trusting when it came to their clients paying for their purchases by cheque. The last time Brittany had visited Pandora, she'd travelled alone and written more than £18,000 in counterfeit cheques. Today she planned on doubling that amount, because after tonight she would be abandoning her grind forever. In the last few weeks, Brittany had hit Lakeside, Birmingham Mall and the West End writing no less than forty dud cheques. The items that she picked up today, minus what she kept for herself, could sell for at least £37,000 on the streets. Her boyfriend Craig's sister, Jessica, who worked in a bank, re-printed customers' cheque books for 40% of Brittany's earnings. Her girlfriend Shelly usually sold most of the women's clothing and accessories to the girls at Sainsburys where she worked. Her customers would snoop around the stores, and then tell Shelly what they wanted. No one could say Brittany's prices weren't negotiable or affordable, but with Craig disappearing off the face of the earth and his sister Jessica not returning any of her calls, Brittany was being forced to put down her pen and retire. Brittany was what she liked to be called, 'Caucasian tanned,' with jet-black hair and a traditional pointy Jewish nose, but her body was shaped like an Afro-Caribbean's. With an all-natural pair of double D's that sat high upon her chest, thick thighs and rounded hips, she had earned the nick name 'Big Booty Britt.' Growing up, her mother had put her weight gain down to the amount of time Brittany spent eating at the Henderson's house next door. "Jerk chicken, green bananas, fried yams, rice and peas are not a normal part of a white girl's diet." Her mother would often mutter this under her breath when Brittany and Sydney would jump the garden fence, climbing from one house to another, getting permission from their parents to spent time at one another's homes after school. "You know those aren't going to fit you right?" said Sydney with raised eyebrows, her hands half tucked in the back pockets of her jeans. She strode over to where Brittany stood with various items of clothing slung over her arm and commented on a pair of jeans Brittany had taken off the sales rack and thrown into her basket. "I know that." Brittany exclaimed. "Most of this shit isn't for me. These jeans are for a customer in Camden. She's a little heavier than me but her waist is kinda small," she whispered putting her basket down and sizing up a pair of custom dark blue denim jeans made by Victoria Beckham next to the ones she wore. "You want me to see if they got 'em in your size?" Brittany said already rummaging through the rack. "I'm telling you Syd, these VB Jeans are what's up right now. And at £468 a pair, it doesn't matter if they fit. A fat bitch could squeeze into a size 10 and have a River Island wearing bitch looking a mess." Sydney glanced at the item and nodded with no reply. She watched as Brittany turned around and continued her weekend ritual of checking labels and sizes before pulling expensive items that neither of them could afford off the shelves, and tossing them in her basket. She knew Brittany's temperament with her over the past few days had been short; Sydney's constant sneaking around and lying generally went unnoticed, but lately it was quite the opposite. Her frame of mind had been unsettled by a disturbing call. 'Maybe it's those fucking green pills, got me hearing all kinds of shit, fucking with my mind,' Sydney thought, as she caught a glimpse of herself in the stores full-length mirror and examined her reflection from afar. She was blessed with features that Brittany couldn't compete with. Sydney's cool chocolate skin complexion was flawless, put together with the dimples indented in her cheeks and her head full of silky, bouncy shoulder-length curls. Plus, add in her thick hips and curves, and there hadn't been a man as far as Sydney could remember that had passed her on the streets without doing a double take. Sydney used to have that 'I can turn a gay man straight before the bitch turns me down' sexiness about her. Though that had been two years ago, it had been a long time since she'd been on the road with her girls, and even longer since she'd been herself. "Thank you for shopping at Pandora Mrs. Havagan, please come again," said the new girl posted at the front desk, shaking Brittany's hand excitedly before she handed her four customized Pandora shopping bags and a receipt. "No, thank you Danni." Brittany said reading the petite girl's name tag. The new store clerk who had come out from the back, and was now posted at the front desk replacing the Ginger who had been so engrossed in the figures she punched in the calculator that she hadn't seen Brittany snatch a stone coloured designer purse from the counter opposite them, nor had she paid attention to the dud cheque Brittany had written out of a near empty cheque book and placed boldly in her hand. Sydney couldn't help but let out short sounds of distress in the small confined space of the elevator. She shifted endlessly where she stood, and repositioned herself twice before the elevator doors opened onto Hampstead Heath's Shopping Centre's ground floor car park. "You know what Syd, I'm done. When we get back to the End's, I'm dropping your ass off at a bus stop unless we pass a cab station on the way outta here. This is stupid and you know it, but if you wanna keep playing this game then fine." Brittany said escaping the crowded elevator crippled with bags. She walked ahead of the two girls in a miserable huff, sucking her teeth loudly for passersby to hear while hurrying herself through the crowd until she was out of Sydney and Shelly's sights. "Damn Syd, what's up with that?" said a shocked Shelly as she turned to Sydney. "Britt!" Shelley called after Brittany, though not loud enough for her to hear. "What the hell's going on between the two of you?" Shelly stopped to ask Sydney again, seeing as her question had gone heard and unanswered the first time she'd asked. Shelly wasn't feisty and loud like Sydney and Brittany, but she knew how to get her claws out and pounce when she found herself surrounded with her back against the wall. Just standing over 5ft with a curvaceous but, stocky frame, Shelly was considered cute-enough. She was reliant on Brittany and Sydney's presence in her life; they were all she had. Sydney's own mother had deliver Special, Shelly's daughter, when she found herself in labor at just thirteen. Shelly looked at Sydney who showed no signs of backing down and decided it was time for her to step in now.

"Should I just assume you're behind all this animosity or are you gonna give it to me straight?" Shelly asked Sydney anticipating her reply. "Brittany saw us last night, we got into it, and now we're just ignoring each other apart from the small talk." Sydney said and sighed, unable to look Shelly directly in the eye. "She knows about you and Judas?" Shelly asked shocked, almost not believing what she'd just heard. "Yeah she knows about me and Judas, I just said she saw us last night didn't I?" Sydney snapped. "Calm down Sydney!" Shelly retorted, feeding Sydney the same attitude she'd fed her. "So, she saw you and Judas together, you know Britt, she ain't gonna remember shit after a few drinks, and it's not like she's gonna go around spreading the word. Who's she gonna tell?" "Brittany's your best friend." Shelly continued whilst she and Sydney began to slowly make their way through the bulk of commuting shoppers towards Brittany's car. "Shelly, don't patronize me. Brittany plays like she's innocent but you know what she's really like. Brittany picks her friends when she needs 'em, and I mean that shit for real. I gave her a bed last night, and when I asked her what the deal was with her not going home, she point blank told me to mind my own business, so when she caught me and Judas hugged up, I dropped the same line and told her to stay outta mines. Fuck knows, why she's trying to be all up in my business now, when she didn't give a damn when I was locked up in Tailsdale or Cleverfield," Sydney replied unfazed. "That's fucked up Syd, you ain't being fair. Brittany dragged her ass to every clinic you were admitted to, she even helped you to escape a number of times, we both did. Brittany ain't the same person she used to be before you were admitted to Cleverfield, you know. Neither of us are, and it's fucked up too, because Brittany's really missed you Syd. Ever since she broke up with Craig..." Shelly began to explain but was interrupted by Sydney's gasp. "Wait," Sydney cut her off before she could say anymore. "Candy Craig!" She giggled like a little girl. "Yeah Candy Craig, but nobody around the way calls him that anymore. It's Cee, and nigga's can't fuck with him like that," Shelly said educating Sydney on the changes in their hood. "Britt and Cee's been together officially for over a year now," Shelley continued. "At first they were just fucking, you know how she does, but then they seemed to be settling down. Britt was feeling Cee differently and Cee must have felt the same because he doesn't let any girls stay where he lays his head, and before he got with Britt I heard he didn't even fuck at his place. Yet, a few months back Cee moved Britt in." Sydney looked at Shelly disbelieving. 'Brittany settling down, yeah right,' she thought. "I'm telling you Syd, they were vibing on a different level. Britt and Craig we're stacking mad paper until some fools from the South or wherever hit him up for his product last week. I took Brittany to the hospital that night, and she's lucky too, because the word on the block is that Cee barely made it out of his flat with his life." "The Hospital," Sydney shrieked, more concerned with Brittany than with Craig. Brittany hardly ever got sick. "She had an abortion Syd, but she didn't want Craig to know. She spent the night in Whipps Cross Hospital because she didn't wanna be spotted at Homerton by anyone in the hood," Shelley whispered. "So what happened to

Craig?" Sydney asked not knowing what to say about Brittany and her decision to terminate her child. "Like I said, I was at the Hospital with Britt, so I don't know. But I do know that Brittany hasn't heard or seen Craig since, and the word on the street is that Brittany called the hit." Again, Shelly lowered her voice as they approached Brittany's car. Sydney opened the door and sat in the passenger's seat despite the tension between Brittany and herself whilst Shelly sat comfortably in the back. "So what's the deal with Craig, I mean Cee?" Sydney turned and whispered to Shelly after Brittany slammed shut the boot. "Do you think Brittany set him up, and pulled this whole abortion stunt to use as an alibi?" she asked while Brittany stood fixing her hair using the reflection of her cars tinted glass. "What? Syd that's sick!" replied Shelly, snapping her neck around to look at Sydney like she was crazy. "I said Cee and Britt were stacking together. Besides, we drove by their flat the following afternoon, and their neighbors said Cee was packed up and gone before the police arrived." "They saw him jump over the fence and run through the back gate while the perpetrators' were straight up busted trying to unscrew Cee's plasma off the wall." Shelly continued as she rested her head on the headrest while Sydney listened, all the while shaking her head. "Brittany just wouldn't do something like that; she's been fucked up about that shit since it went down." "Damn, I don't blame her." Sydney finally said. "I can't even imagine Craig on his grind, let alone Brittany fucking with him and them both getting it in." "You're telling me the truth right, Craig and Brittany?" Sydney quietly laughed to herself, and then turned her attention to her window as Brittany seemed to be having some kind of bitter discussion with the security guard they'd greeted outside Pandora. "Ah wah ya ave fa mi Brit-Annie?" said the West Indian sounding security guard, as he licked his lips smiling and showing a grill full of rotten teeth. He used a soiled, white cloth to wipe the sweat dripping from his brow, before placing it in his back pocket where he'd taken it from. The Bernie Mac looking man wheezed heavily, looked Brittany up and down, and then stuck his hand out waiting for Brittany to put in his palm the only thing his heart desired, and their reason for visiting Hampstead Heath's Shopping Centre this afternoon. "Freddie put your fucking hand down." Brittany snapped, shaking her head in disbelief. She surveyed the parking lot discreetly to make sure no one was eyeing her before reaching into her purse and retrieving the small rock of cocaine the crack addict security guard had been pestering her for all day. She held the last of her stash in the palm of her hand. "Fred, there's a situation up here that needs your attention." A voice called from the guard's walkie-talkie. Quickly, Freddie grabbed the rock out of Brittany's hand and shoved it deep into his front pocket before detaching his walkie- talkie from his waist band and turning to leave. "Excuse me!" Brittany shrieked, with her hand held out, "My money you fat fuck!" she called after him. "Put your fucking hand down," Freddie laughed making his way through the crowd before Brittany could get another word in. He muttered something about a warning and it going before destruction, but it was something Brittany didn't care to hear as she composed herself and got into her car determined to put Freddie, and her crack selling days behind her. "What the hell Brittany!" shouted Shelly in protest, at the way Brittany had slammed her car door shut, thrown herself in the driver's seat and frantically pushed the key in the ignition of her cherry red Audi A3, then stuck her head out the window as she backed out of her space. "Move out the fucking way or imma back the fuck into your car!" She yelled out, banging on the steering wheel at the fools who thought they'd have a better chance of getting into her space if they waited up her ass. Brittany revved her engine to let the people behind her know she was reversing, and that she had no problem fucking up their ride. She looked up into her rear-view mirror, and cursed when she noticed the ginger-headed clerk from Pandora standing on the second floor pointing her car out to a set of security guards heading their way. Freddie was hot on her heels too. "Syd look in your mirror, and tell me that I'm not paranoid?" Brittany asked, wanting to get her opinion. "You're not paranoid Britt, their on to us." Sydney reported back, and sunk down in her seat. She began to panic seeing the guards making their way down the escalators, heading towards them. It almost reminded her of those nights in Cleverfield when she'd attempted to escape. She closed her eyes in an attempt to drown out the noise. "Back the fuck up!" Brittany frantically screamed out of her window to a 'Good Samaritan' who had attempted to block them in. The bald headed man did as he was told just seconds before one of the guards grabbed, and tried to pull open the passenger side door. "I suggest you stop this right now before this gets worse than it needs to be," a heavy built security guard commanded, but Brittany wasn't having any of it. She backed out of her parking space and headed towards the nearest exit, hitting the highway at full speed.

Chapter 3

"WHAT?" yelled Judas into the mouthpiece of his apartment's cordless phone. He was still half asleep when the private caller had rung, stopped, and then rung again, determined to wake him up. "It's nice to hear from you too Judas. Did I catch you at a bad time?" spat Stitches, the mother of his youngest-child, with venom at him through the phone. Judas sighed, rubbing the sleep from his eyes as he looked towards his nightstand, reading the time on the digital clock that sat beside a picture of him and his fiancée Naomi on their recent vacation to the South of France. "You need to stop doing this Stitches," spoke Judas calmly into the phone. Stitches had recently started playing mind games with him and Naomi by calling and hanging up on their home phone in an attempt to wind Naomi up, which usually had Judas fired up and banging on her door. "Stop what Judas? Stop feeding your daughter? Tameerah hasn't seen you in a week. What do you think she eats, fresh fucking air?" Stitches rhetorically asked, and Judas could have sworn he felt her smile through the phone. Judas had first met Stitches when he rushed his man Sticks to

Homerton Hospital after he'd been stabbed and was admitted into ICU. Back then Stitches was a student-nurse, and was training in Homerton Hospital in the emergency ward, stitching up and tending to patients minor wounds. Judas had been cut during the brawl, but had refused to be treated; he had to be on point for Sticks. He didn't have time to play 21 questions with the doctors or the police. Stitches had come across as a gullible, but well educated university student, innocent to the world, though she lived and worked in the heart of the hood. Her 'no questions asked' mentality was what had drawn Judas to her from the jump. Stitches had taken Judas home that very night, stitched him up, and then giggled like a schoolgirl when he gave her the nickname 'Stitches' after gratefully admiring her work. She was Nurse Reid by day and Stitches by night. It wasn't long before Stitches was upgraded from Judas's bed to a permanent position on his payroll. Now she stitched up and cleaned the wounds of various criminals who were wealthy enough to pay Judas for her trade. Her clients entered her ground floor flat through the back door into her kitchen, and after she got to work on them, Judas would go to work on her. At twenty-two Stitches had a figure that should have been oiled down and showcased in a magazine. It was almost impossible for Judas to resist hitting it from behind at least once, after watching her bend over to attend to his bleeding wound. Stitches was a car crash in the bedroom and her head game was D.O.A. She worked her ass off for Judas, but her unexpected pregnancy took the fun out of whatever it was she assumed they had. "What can I do for you Stitches?"

Judas asked in his 'Don't fuck with me' tone. "I miss you Judas, we both miss you. It's not even about the money." Stitches admitted. Judas had promised Stitches a lifetime together, their seven-year-old daughter was approaching eight and had yet to see even 24 hours with the man she called dad. "Look Stitches, you need to stop pushing this bullshit idea of us being together," Judas said reaching out for the framed photo on the nightstand beside his bed. Stitches had been getting on Naomi's last nerve with her games, and she was starting to get on Judas's nerves too. "Why do we have to put a label on what we got and call it a family?" Judas asked. He loved the sexual energy he had with Stitches, but hated the hold she had on him when it came to their child. Judas held on to the picture frame and looked into the face of his first love. "Because we are a family Judas, we don't have a choice in this matter. You are Tameerah's father, and she's your child, unfortunately, she deserves your love." Stitches pronounced in her defense. "Well I can't do it." Judas said point blankly, and placed the photo on the bed. He sat up straight, and yawned aloud. "I make sure you and my daughter are nice don't I? What more do you want?" "Sending strange men to our house at all hours of the night is not making sure we're nice!" Stitches said in frustration and sniffed. "What happened to keeping us safe, you just giving out my address now? Nigga's pay for their treatment and you tell them where?" She sobbed. "Stitches you know I can't be up and down in these streets, I ain't got time to be running people by your house when their hot. I ain't going to jail for some bullshit neither," Judas explained with a sly smile of his own.

"Bullshit!" shouted Stitches. "Come on girl, you know what I mean. Swishing your ass around in your shorts around them dope boys that roll through after a throw down," Judas smirked. He knew Stitches would be racking her brain trying to find out how he knew about that incident seeing as they were classified customers of her own. "It's all good Stitches, you do you." Judas chuckled. "Get that money how you need to get it during the week, and I'll see you at my mother's house on Sunday afternoon." "You know what, fuck you Judas," Stitches sulked, "Your mother's house is like a sauna and your other baby momma's get on my damn nerves, especially that Keion." "Hello!" She shouted after realizing Judas hadn't responded in a while. "Are you even listening to me?" "Yeah I'm listening to you Stitches, I just don't care. I'm about fed up with all this Sunday lunch crap as much as you women are, but Tameerah, Shayanne, Brooklyn, Ameerah and Kayla are sisters, so get over it!" Judas spat. "There ain't shit I can do about the situation but deal with it." Stitches disconnected the call. "Stupid bitch," Judas muttered, and then sat silent hearing that the line was still open and hadn't gone dead. "Hello, Judas," a voice of authority said through the open line. "Who's dat...?" Judas cautiously asked. "It's your father you ugly shit, but you would have known that if you hadn't had me waiting on the other line for so god-damned long." Judas heard his father bellow into the phone. "Dad, what's up? I didn't even hear the other line beep." "Look... I know what you're gonna say, but just let me explain?" Judas sat up straight and adjusted his position on the bed. He and his father ran a lucrative theft and laundering operation within the Metropolitan Law enforcement. Since joining the Force, his father, Sensi Mendez had been involved in 27 raids since November of '99. One of which resulted in the murder of Gerald Hastings, and another in connection to the fall of the Henderson's reign. Sensi was one of four officers assigned to the Henderson Case. After ginning up a story to obtain a search warrant to the Henderson's home address, Sensi had his team do a no-knock entry, which resulted in an officer shooting and wounding the leader. The officers then planted heroin in their basement and asked another informant to lie on the enforcement's behalf in an attempt to cover up their intentions. Two officers pled guilty to county charges of voluntary manslaughter and a charge of violating constitutional rights. They were currently sitting in county prisons, both serving 7 year sentences. Detective Greenham, the only one to go to trial, had been prosecuted and charged with the lesser crime of making a false statement to an investigator and violating his oath of office. Greenham faced up to 16 years in prison if convicted, leaving his position wide open for the taking. Sensi was highly praised by his team, who were oblivious to the fact he was a street informant. He'd instantly seized the opportunity presented before him, and soon enough was promoted to Major on his own technicalities. A male protagonist by all accounts, Detective Mendez had the district eating out of his hands. When he'd cunningly informed the law enforcement community about the Henderson's profitable drug activity, whilst manipulating other officers to step out of their line of duty, he'd masterfully dictated both sides. The Henderson's were ruthless in their dealings and Sensi despised the fact that they had members of law enforcement on their payroll, something that just wasn't going to happen on his watch. When the dust had settled, and the transfer was made, the Superintendent of London was singing Sensi's praises for his work on the investigation and helping to bring down Hackney's most notorious drug lords. Detective Greenham's participation in the conspiracy had law enforcement using him as a prime example to any other officer thinking about manipulating the system. The Superintendent made plans to have him publicly humiliated then sent to prison to rot, but Greenham had other ideas. Determined not to go down without a fight, Greenham sought the expertise of a private investigator, and dug up an incriminating past during an enhanced background check against Sensi and the other three officers involved in the corruption case. Unfortunately for him, his investigator was killed in a fatal road crash whilst on his way to report his findings. Greenham was sentenced to 13 years in prison under the constitutional rights law, where he only lasted six months. Sensi had known it wouldn't be long before Greenham's body would be found hanging from the light cord in his cell, and he was right. Sensi parked his car crookedly beside a parking inspector, rolled down his window, and opened his glove compartment to retrieve a cigar he had lusted after since breakfast this morning. His current piece of ass was asthmatic, and would be coughing and spitting at even the slightest hint of smoke. "I'm listening," he said. He rolled his eyes while leaning back in his seat and preceded to light his cigar with the car's built in lighter. It was predictable for Judas to let his temperament get the better of him, ending all possible logical thought, and causing him to fail where instructions were concerned. "I fucked up dad, I know. But in my defense I didn't know that was your raid, I didn't even know you had any of my guys under investigation," Judas said doubting his father even knew how he operated on the streets. "Craig's been walking around with his pockets full for some time now, and I figured it was time I reminded him who was boss," he explained agitated. "By sending three incompetent rough-necks to rob him before a federal raid," replied sarcastically while Sensi coughing and shifting in his seat. He sat parked two buildings down from the local picture house awaiting the beginning of his show. "Is it not enough that you're the sole distributor of this district? Are you not content with the status you hold?" Sensi asked. "Your stupidity landed three files on my desk and a whole bunch of questions that I have to make go away. Honestly Judas, it is imperative that you have these dealers in your debt. You're constantly competing in your own competitions, setting the bar just high enough for you to reach and for everybody else to touch. Judas, one day you'll realize that power is not strength but numbers. Now is not the time for a war, not whilst were living good." Sensi advised remembering how little power he'd held during the Henderson's reign. Sensi knew more about the streets than he cared for his son to know. He also knew first hand that it was better to be the power behind the scenes, than to be the icon of your trade.

Chapter 4

Essen casually strode towards a hefty ticket attendant in Rio's picture-house dressed in a rugged pair of black Levis, a simple black t-shirt covered by a baseball jacket, and a crisp black pair of Air Force Ones on his feet. He handed the woman his ticket, and waited to be shown to his screen. "Thank you Sir, its screen four right ahead," the cheerful woman instructed, taking his ticket and letting him through the double screen doors. He held a large bag of popcorn under his arm, a large plastic disposable cup of Coke in one hand, and with his free hand, he held the screen door open for a group of teenage girls who giggled when they bounced past him popping their gum. Essen entered the screen with ease, and seeing that the film's adverts had started and most of the seats were full except for a few at the back, vigilantly slipped into the shadows, and snuck into a side chair close to the screens exit next to a brother who clapped his hands, obviously hyped by the trailer of a film. Forty minutes into the film and the ambiance in the room was tense. The sounds of guns blazing while actor Denzel Washington fought a feud in his latest film, 'American

Gangster' had the audience in awe. Essen seized his opportunity to shuffle down in his chair and drop two seats below, stopping beside his mark in the dark. He moved into the shadows where he couldn't be seen and screwed the silencer onto his 6 inch Colt Python Revolver, which he had kept hidden in his popcorn bag until now. The Python was his old friend. He stood inches away from his victim, watching as the actors continued to eliminate their opponents before he fired a single shot, catching his victim dead in the throat. The man's head fell to the side, and he caught a glimpse of his killer before gurgling and grunting on his own blood, and struggling to take his last breath. Essen looked up at the screen again to see the bloodshed and mayhem was over, much like the life of his victim. "Their dropping like flies man," the two hundred pound brother beside Essen chuckled; he had slipped back into his seat unnoticed, and was sitting sipping at his coke through a straw. Both men shared a few friendly words then continued to watch the film until the credits rolled up and the lights came on. "Nah, that film was serious," the man said, turning to Essen before getting up to leave, only to find that he'd already slipped out. "Wankster," he chuckled to himself as he was being escorted out of the building by one of the many police officers strangely filling up the screen. Essen watched from car parked across the street as the police rounded up the majority of screen four for questioning before turning his attention to the young girl who trembled uncontrollably in another officer's arms. The teenager had spent the last half hour next to her father's lifeless body, and was now covered in seventy percent of his blood from her struggle with the paramedics when she'd begged them to revive him, though he was pronounced dead at the scene. Essen had turned his attention away from the scene for a second, when the real action started. "DROP YOUR BAG NOW!" An armed, uniformed, officer shouted ready to fire on command. The two hundred pound brother held his hands up high above his head, and immediately dropped the contents he held, causing the gun that Essen had placed with him to fire, flattening the tire of a marked police vehicle. "I ain't done anything man; I swear, I ain't ever seen that thing before," he roared as he was restrained to the ground. People looked on as armed officers surrounded him with their weapons drawn, praying they'd get the chance to dissemble his body in the streets. "You enjoying the show boy?" Sensi crept up and asked with sarcasm, snapping Essen out of his thoughts. Sensi stood at 6ft, and was broad shouldered much like his son. Sensi and Judas were so much alike, that the only thing to define the two was age. Judas had that 'good-hair' women prayed their children would inherit as did Sensi, and they both shared the same dashing smile casing a row of perfect white teeth. A whole generation before signing up for his badge, Sensi was known as the right-hand man of one of the most respected men in East London, Andy Henderson AKA Lock-Ness. Lock-Ness and Sensi went way back, as far as their late teens. Sensi was the mind and muscle behind Lock's hood fame, and in his opinion, all Lock had was charm. Still, they were boys, and together they started a lucrative drug operation, posing as respectable businessmen while trafficking heroin and cocaine through the district of the East End. But after years of violence and bloodshed, Lock-Ness claimed the top spot in town, cementing his legend in the hood. No amount of food moved in or out of East London without Sensi or Lock's OK. However, Sensi had other plans. He grew tired of being passed off as some old has-been bodyguard. Exchanging his player's card for a shiny badge made him the real boss in his hometown, but his actions caused havoc all around Hackney. And when word got back to Lock-Ness that his boy was working for the feds, his comrades on the streets grew angry with betrayal. Sensi had won over a small part of the town and had lived lavishly until he'd eaten up his stash and was left with two options, live cheque to cheque, or crawl back to his ex-partner in crime. At the time, Sensi had cringed at the idea of groveling to Lock. But what was a little animosity between friends? Sensi approached Lock with a humble heart; he explained that it would be beneficial for them to do business together again and, how convenient it was to have friends in high places. "For you brother, I can get you first-hand information on raids, investigations, provide you with federal weapons and even..." Armor, was what Sensi was about to say, before Lock spat in his face. He damn near ripped off his badge in disgust, raving to his surrounding crew, who already had their hands on their machines in case Sensi felt brave, that Sensi had completely sold out, and the only reprieve Lock had promised him for his betrayal was a slow death. "There are no friends in the feds, just snitches." Lock had spat. Today, Sensi could hold his head up high and smile. 'Had he taken up my offer that armor would have come in handy.' He chuckled his way into a cough. "You alright Mr. M?" Essen asked, unlocking the passenger door for the detective to take a seat. Together they sat in silence watching the scene before them unfold. "Congratulations." Sensi finally said, not once taking his eyes off the scene. "I didn't wanna say anything before because I thought it might throw you off your game, but the man you just assassinated was Jeffrey Perkins." The Detective coughed again before retrieving his inhaler from his pocket. 'Jeffrey Perkins,' Essen thought, knowing he'd heard the name before, but couldn't quite place the acquaintance. Essen thought hard. "I'm not following," he replied confused. He watched the detective place his inhaler between his lips and struggle for air, before placing it securely back in his pocket to put in its place a cigar. Essen turned his attention back to the scene, making eye contact with the fifteen-year-old daughter of the deceased. He now had a recollection of Jeffrey Perkins. He knew exactly who he had been ordered to kill.

Chapter 5

"**S**o bitch, you gonna tell me when you started fucking Judas or am I gonna have to catch you two butt naked again to find out?" Brittany asked, as she looked through her front mirror, in attempt to put an end to their awkwardness which had lasted during their journey back to Hackney from Hampstead Heath. "Who said me and Judas were fucking? What you saw last night kinda just happened." Sydney objectively replied. "Forget all that 'it just happened shit' Syd, I know fucking when I see it, and you two were throwing it down. Your ass and titties was bouncing around like you were in a porno." Brittany laughed, as did Sydney and Shelly from the backseat. "Sydney was putting it down, and I mean putting it down Shell!" Brittany teased, bouncing up and down in her seat. "Stop it." Sydney screamed embarrassed by Brittany's recount of her sexual encounter with the man she'd fallen in love with. "You need to be minding your own damn business instead of minding mine..." "Okay, so we're judging each other now yeah?" Brittany said making a right at the roundabout into the London Borough of Hackney. "I'm just saying." Sydney went on. "You're fucking a drug dealer too, and you got the nerve to sit there and comment about who I'm fucking." Brittany stopped at a red light and turned to Shelly, "Is she serious?" she asked, not caring so much that Shelly had discussed her dealings with Craig to Sydney, but amazed that Sydney thought she could compare the two. "I'm sorry Syd, remind us again how me dating Craig, 'yes a drug dealer,' outweighs you fucking your sister's man?" Brittany demanded to know. Sydney didn't reply, though she knew Brittany would go there, that was the reason she'd kept her involvement with Judas from her in the first place. "That's right Syd you can't." Brittany said putting her Audi A3 into fourth gear. "I've pulled some real shysty shit over the years, but this one deserves a round of applause." "She's right you know Syd," Shelly spoke up from the backseat "I don't even wanna think about how Naomi's gonna react when she finds out your sleeping with her man." "You think that's bad?" Brittany said pulling up on her road, preparing to park outside her house. "We're gonna look like some real heartless bitches when all this comes out. Naomi's your daughter's God-mother; how you think she's gonna feel knowing you helped her sister stab her in the back?" Brittany said, as she turned to Shelly, as if Sydney wasn't sitting in the next seat. "Fuck you Britt!" Sydney sulked, releasing herself from her seat belt, getting out the car, and slamming the door shut. While her secret was safe with Shelly, Sydney wasn't so sure it was safe with Brittany. "Welcome home bitch." Brittany smirked Sydney's way as pushed her key in her front door. She waddled up the stairs into her home, using her right foot to force open her bedroom door and relieve herself of the bags and packages filled with the items she'd purchased at Hampstead Heath Shopping centre earlier that day. Her room, the master bedroom, was painted a pearl peach. The four poster bed, situated in the middle of the room against the textured wall, was the main attraction. It was draped in gold and peach coloured linens, piled with cream and gold cushions and pillows, all neatly made under a cream coloured canopy that hung above the beams. To the left of the room sat her dressing table, filled with perfumes, nail varnishes and all other types of female products one would find on their boudoir. To the right stood a large fireplace, as did each and every other master bedroom in the old Victorian style houses, which resided on Queensbridge Road. Brittany's bedroom reminded Sydney of her parents' bedroom, which would have been right next-door. It had large bay windows, an Aertex ceiling and the fireplace was her father's favorite feature. Sydney often found him staring into the flames deep in thought. Nevertheless, while the layout remained a memory, the décor and furnishings represented Brittany to a tee. Besides the usual clutter and over flowing clothes hamper, the only things that stood out of place were the piles of unopened merchandise all purchased and paid for by Brittany's hustle. "I see you finally got your room, huh?" Sydney said entering Brittany's bedroom, shaking her head at the thought of Brittany's parents giving up their room. She threw herself on the bed, sitting upright between the mountains of cushions and kicked off her shoes exposing her perfectly manicured feet. "Yeah she got her room alright," said Shelly, with both hands struggling to hold on to the bags she helped Brittany bring in from the car. "Can you believe her parents didn't even put up a fight? One minute Brittany was complaining that her room was too small, and the next we were picking wallpaper?" She laughed. Brittany paid the girls no mind. Instead, she walked across the room to her nightstand, and taking off a key which she wore around her neck on a chain, she opened the small drawer and placed inside the three cheque books she'd made purchases with that afternoon. Jessica hadn't called her all day. In fact, she hadn't returned any of Brittany's calls since her brother disappeared. Maybe it was time to pay her a visit. "I'm officially broke!" she announced after re-locking her side-drawer and plopping down on the bed beside Sydney. If Craig wanted to break it off with her, FINE, she'd find herself another sucker to scam off of. She told herself this daily, but Brittany was never good at deceiving herself with lies. Craig had taken more than their stash when he left her; he'd taken her heart. Money could be remade or replaced but her heart demanded answers, and maybe even revenge. Brittany was fast growing tired of black men fucking her over like she didn't have to work just as hard for her shit like everybody else. Shelly watched as Brittany recovered her weed stash, emptied the contents onto the bed and started to strap up. That was her exit. Brittany had been tripping over Craig long enough, and Shelly didn't understand why she was so fucked up over him bouncing when she'd told her she was planning on baling on him her damn self. Shelly was leaving, but not without her money. "Syd, I'm gone. Watch her for me, and call me?" Sydney knew what Shelly meant. Brittany was so busy satisfying her mind that she didn't even notice Shelley slip out her room with her bags. Shelly didn't have the time to wait for Brittany to get her mind straight before she conducted business like she would on any other given day. Unlike Sydney and Brittany, Shelly had responsibilities. Her thirteen year old daughter, Special, would be up waiting for her to come home, and this little hustle was protecting her ass. Brittany wouldn't even miss the items in the bags she'd taken; she had most of the items with labels still on them cluttered around her room. If anything, she'd make Brittany understand. After all, what was a little hostility between friends?

Chapter 6

Shelly hurried two steps at a time down the stairs towards the basement in the three-bedroom house that she and her daughter had been made to call home. She'd known from the moment she arrived at Gatwick airport, that Angela, her father's wife, had hated the fact that her husband's bitch had sent their love child to live in their home. Angela had made no effort what so ever to accept Shelly as a part of her family. Instead she allowed her son, who at the time of her arrival was eighteen, to sexually abuse her when their father wasn't around. "I know you got some cash for me in these pockets, you tight bitch," Bradley said while he frantically searched and rummaged through the dirty clothing Shelly had stepped out of before she'd gotten in the shower. "I need a drink, God damn-it," he shouted becoming enraged. He knew if he dug deep enough in Shelly's pockets he'd get what he was searching for and sure enough just as he was about to give up he felt a lump in the back pocket of Shelly's jeans. "I knew you had something for me." Bradley said, almost foaming at the mouth as he pulled at the shower curtain and grinned. He fixed his eyes on Shelly's naked body, soaped up and dripping wet, and suddenly a drink was the last thing on his mind. He followed the drops of water as they fell from the showerhead, down her shoulders, her back, between the crack of her ass and swiftly down her legs. "Bradley, please. Just take the money and leave me alone." Shelly pleaded, stiffening from the cold and the sight of Bradley's manhood rising in his pants. Bradley stood stuffing the neatly folded notes that Shelly had tried her hardest to hide into his own pocket. He still anticipated a drink, but his desire to molest his half-sister was the hardest addiction he'd yet to try and fight. "You don't mind do you?" Bradley pointed to the toilet. Shelly nodded 'No,' but cringed as Bradley lifted the toilet seat and relieved himself in her presence. He kept his eyes on Shelly's body, though she had covered what little she could with her hands since she felt exposed. Afraid to move, she feared what was to come next as she had been through the nightmare several times before. After flushing the toilet, Bradley stood erect and exposed. Without wiping or even shaking off his dick, he slowly approached the shower which Shelly stood inside and began to stroke his erection until she did what he wanted. She begged. "Please Bradley," Shelly's voice quivered as she watched Bradley's manhood grow long and hard. "Not while Special's in the house," she begged, but her begging fell on deaf ears. Bradley, with his pants at his ankles, pleasured himself whilst Shelly thought of a route of escape. She knew if worst came to worst he'd have her bent over the sink in a strong hold, whilst he penetrated her from behind. At least that way she could keep the door shut to prevent Special from walking in. Shelly didn't notice the expression on Bradley's face had turned from rape to rage, nor did she notice that he had long stepped out his pants until he was up beside her naked, reeking of alcohol, ass and weed. "No...Ouch No..!" Shelly yelped when Bradley twisted her arm behind her back and pushed her up against the bathroom wall. She struggled to break free whilst Bradley struggled to get her into a more compromising position. Shelly kept her eyes on the door as Bradley began to violate her vigorously. She half wished someone would rush in on them, exposing Bradley for the rapist he was, but unfortunately for Shelly, no one caught Bradley during his act of molestation; just like they hadn't caught him yesterday or the day before. Shelly had reached the bottom of the stairs out of breath and exhausted, when she flung open the basement door and froze. Bradley stood bent over Special as she sat around the small, round dining table dimly lit by a lamp. Both of them were engaged in conversation and unaware of Shelly's presence while she stood in the doorway unable to move. "What the hell is going on in here?" her voice quivered as she spoke. She could only hold onto the frame of the door to keep her legs from going under. "We're doing geography mum," Special said, quickly, and straightened up hearing her mother's voice. Shelly said nothing. She stared at Bradley as he stood looking over his shoulder grinning. "I was struggling, and it's gotta be handed-in in the morning," Special moaned. She knew her mother was strict about homework, and after school activities. Special took up gymnastics, dance, swimming, and could play the piano almost as good a Stevie Wonder himself. Shelly had enrolled Special in anything that kept her out of the house whilst she had to work, but days like this were inevitable. "I'll catch up with you another time baby-girl," Bradley said high-fiving his niece. "You come find me if you ever find yourself struggling, okay?" he alleged in a way, which to Shelly, implied her daughter had gone to him because she simply wasn't there. "You can thank me later yeah," Bradley whispered when he slipped past Shelly at the basement door, and ascended up the stairs into the house. Shelly stepped closer to the bottom of the stairs, and waited until she heard the opening of a beer can, and the TV switch on before she hurried into the basement and secured the door behind her. "That was soo rude," said Special. Shelly turned to see her almost fourteen-year-old daughter looking at her the same way she'd looked at Sydney that day; like she'd lost her damned mind. Special was growing up fast, her round face and fair-skinned complexion resembled Shelly's own, but everything else came unmistakably from her dad. "It wasn't rude." Shelly brushed her daughter off. "When I said I didn't want anybody down here I meant it." "Yeah I know, lock the door when you get back and lock the door when you leave. This is bullshit mum, Uncle Bradley lives in the same house as us!" Special cursed, throwing her pen down in a sulk. She kicked the base of the table and folded her arms, obviously upset but determined not to cry. "It's how it has to be Special!" Shelly stressed without an explanation. She excused her daughter's foul mouth because she understood her need to express herself. "But it's not fair!" Special sobbed, now in her mother's arms. "I know it's not fair baby." Shelly held her daughter close, trying to hold back tears of her own. Special was imprisoned by her mother's fears, and had lived that way all her life. The basement was their sanctuary, the only place in the house safe enough to keep Bradley out. Shelly had spent thousands of pounds reconstructing the moldy room into a livable den. Angela had made it crystal clear that under no circumstances did she want Special under her roof. Her suspicions of Bradley's fertility sickened her, yet she was forced to blame herself for the consequence of her ignorance. She almost threw a fit when the IKEA builders delivered, and fitted a brand new wall kitchen and open bathroom suite into the lower level of her house. The basement, an open room at the bottom of the house, gave Shelly a lot of room to play with. But it wasn't enough. She wanted a real home, with windows, and doors, and a bedroom for Special to call her own. Ever since, the builders had come and gone, Angela had started to charge rent. She figured if Shelly could afford to pay for luxuries, then she could afford to pay her way. Fortunately for Shelly her father was man enough to object to Angela's cruelty, but there were still other things Angela could charge Shelly for. And right now she was extorting her for two hundred and fifty pounds a week to keep Bradley out her daughter's draws.

Chapter 7

Naomi aggressively ripped open the budget packaging of a home pregnancy kit, and pulled both sticks out the packet. She placed one on top of the counter beside the sink, and somehow in all the excitement managed to drown the other stick like instructed, while urinating on her fingers at the same time. 'WAIT 3 MINUTES FOR RESULTS,' the instructions on the packet read, though the case clearly stated that the results would be immediate. Standing up to straighten her clothes, Naomi noticed something strange swimming at the bottom of the bowl. Nah, that can't be what I think it is? She thought as she watched the pieces of toilet paper separate in the water she had just urinated in to reveal a bloated yellow condom. "This child is too much!" Naomi cursed out loud. Sucking her teeth, she closed the toilet seat and stood on the lid, level with the medicine cabinet above the sink. She placed the pregnancy stick upright on top of the cabinet, jumped down from the toilet, grabbed her purse off the counter, and stuffed all the other pregnancy test contents in it before pulling out her phone. "The mobile phone you have called is switched off. Please call again later." The automated operator replied each time Naomi dialed Sydney's phone. Sheer curiosity made her open the bathroom door and look around the apartment. Bare footed, Naomi walked towards the lounge, and stumbled on yet another piece of evidence to suggest that foul play had been going on under her roof. Naomi picked up the empty condom wrapper that was on the arm of the recliner and headed straight towards Sydney's room. Twice she knocked and waited, but no one answered. The flicker of light coming from under the door indicated that Sydney was indeed home, her lack of respect was noted, and Naomi did what she felt was necessary. "What the fuck Naomi, you gonna break the fucking door?" Sydney said, having jumped out of a light, scared half to death after hearing her bedroom door being kicked in. "What's wrong with you?" Sydney asked, seeing Naomi standing in her doorway ready to pounce with her hair slightly out of place. Only once had Sydney seen Naomi with her hair a mess; scratch that, twice. The first time was when their father was killed, and the last was when they were taken into foster care. "Don't, what's wrong with me Sydney, look at this shit!" Naomi stormed into Sydney's bedroom, and dangled the empty condom wrapper in her face. Judas was highly favored in the streets, and as much as he had friends he had enemies. Naomi had stressed the importance of keeping their whereabouts low-key to Sydney a number of times. Not that they had anything incriminating to hide, it was just how Judas liked it, and how you lived when you ran in the streets. "What's the point in talking to you Sydney, when you think everything I say is a joke?" Naomi said talking to her sister's reflection as her bed faced a large built-in, mirrored wardrobe. Sydney sat up, wiping her mouth and glaring back at the only person in the world that could have saved her from the nightmares she'd endured when they lost their parents. Except deep down, she knew she didn't deserve to be saved. She was falling hard for her sister's future husband. Naomi had seemed so happy when she'd told Sydney about her upcoming wedding. Officially, after twelve years, both she and Judas were finally planning on tying the knot. Sydney felt a surge of guilt invade her sprit, but she was accustomed to the feeling. No matter what her mind told her, her heart loved Judas more and she knew that no matter what the situation, she'd be with him till the very end. Naomi eventually left Sydney alone, and proceeded on her way to the master bedroom where she found Judas snoring lightly in his sleep. He was fully clothed unlike when she'd left him before she made her rounds in the morning, and the keys to his BMW X4 were settled on the side table next to a stack of fifty's, indicating he'd been out handling his business in the streets. The air in the room was quilted with light smoke, so Judas must have dosed off a little before she arrived. "Lucky for Syd it was me who found her shit, or Judas would have hit the fan," Naomi thought out loud as she undressed. Judas had become quite protective of Sydney since she'd moved into their apartment, but it was expected of any good man after knowing the pain and distraught the poor girl had been through. Naomi sat down on the plush bedding that covered her queen-sized bed and kicked off her five inch heels. She was pleased with her position in life and felt quite blessed. She'd managed to recreate herself, detaching herself from the stories the streets told of her unfortunate family name. Her father's death was just the beginning of the terrible events that had helped change her before she met Judas. Before her father's death, the world had been a carefree place with her daddy attending to her heart's every desire. Naomi was the heart of his world, and he in return, was the center of hers. Without her father, Naomi was exposed to the dangers of a world she once thought she owned. Confident in her own right, Naomi had dominated the girls around the way, even as a teenager. Because of her daddy, she was named best dressed four years in a row and hottest student in the fall of 98'. But now she felt betrayed. Her father hadn't deserved the betrayal his hometown delivered him at his fall and neither did her family. Like scavenger's, they were left to beg and demand what was owed to them from Andy's previous clients, and people the family had once considered good friends. At just thirteen Naomi watched her mother go from the strong, attractive woman she was, to a mere description of a human being. Just two years prior to her husband's death, Whitney had devoured her family's assets, (at least what was left of it) and the police had seized all properties believed to be purchased unlawfully, and blocked all accounts in the Henderson name. Naomi vowed that if she had to take anything from her father's death it would be a lesson well learnt. She was fully aware of Judas's line of work but cared more for the future they'd spent years planning together, than for the financial joys his street life gave. At 29, Naomi would swear that before she went to bed at night, when the house and the world outside of her window was asleep, she could hear her body's clock ticking, and often feared she'd be left having children to late. Judas and Naomi shared a three bedroom, one level apartment on Oakland Due Avenue that Naomi, of course had furnished with nothing but the finest in designer furnishings. Together they co-owned two thriving businesses, two properties, including their apartment, and a residential building named Bowma Tower in Islington, Old Street. Sure, Naomi was ambitious and successful but she was the epitome of today's modern woman; personally handling the accounts to all the businesses and their Residential Block, Naomi's administrative skills far out weighted Judas' with little competition. Her one true flaw was loneliness, and this attribute made her vulnerable. Any man she let near her heart could do with it as he pleased, virtually having his way with her as a result. In the solitude of her own room, Naomi stepped out of her knitted Christian Dior dress and placed it neatly across the chaise. She un-clipped her bracelets from around her wrists and placed them on the dresser along with her matching diamond clustered earrings before stepping into her newly refurbished en-suite. Inside, she allowed her day to conclude and released a mixture of emotions through tears. She had long forgotten about the pregnancy test she had taken before she was distracted by her sister's foul play. Judas changed his position on the queen-sized bed, and slightly opened his eyes to the muffled sounds coming from his en suite. Pretending to be asleep was the only way he'd been able to stay out of the war that had become a daily occurrence between the two women he shared his home with. ARE YOU OK? Judas typed into his blackberry, selecting Syd from his contact list, and then pressing 'Send.' BETTER KNOWING YOUR THINKIN BOUT ME, Sydney immediately replied. Judas smiled, and then frowned when Naomi entered the master bedroom, in a bathrobe, her body still wet and glistening under the bedroom's dim light. She'd tried her best to conceal the sounds of her frustration whilst she bathed, but her swollen eyes were a total give away that she'd been crying, something Judas had rarely seen, but often heard her do. "Nay, what's wrong?" Judas softly asked. His phone beeped again but he ignored it, tucking it under his pillow as he watched his woman standing with her back to him. Her creamy skin was somewhat hypnotizing him with the calming scent from her lavender and vanilla body oils. It had been less than an hour since he'd been with her sister, yet he couldn't control the reaction of his manhood if he tried, to what he knew was under Naomi's robe. "Would you get my back for me baby?" Naomi sweetly asked. She'd deliberately ignored Judas's question, just like he'd ignored his phone. Naomi had known all about the girls Judas had fucked around with in the past, and though she didn't like it, she respected the way he handled his, stepping up to his responsibilities and never denying his children. Naomi sat between Judas's legs on the bed while he took his time applying the sweet-smelling lotion onto her back. He then used the palms of his hands to gently rub it into her skin. "Ummm right there," Naomi threw her head back and mumbled as Judas worked his fingers into the creases of her back. It hadn't proved easy managing a business and a rental property single-handed, but Judas had forewarned her of the responsibility before she'd had him invest. It didn't matter that her girl Samantha helped her manage the Salon, or that they'd employ half a dozen staff. Chasing tenants took time, and so did chasing Judas' loud-mouthed, worthless baby mothers off her premises. 'I can just hear them now; Oh lawd, Judas got another baby out there in the streets. Naomi needs to let that Nigga go,' she imagined her stylist Stacey saying. Judas began caressing her waist, slowly heading south. Fortunately, it was all in her mind, but there was always something to preoccupy her when it came to spending with time and satisfying her man. Judas hadn't touched her in over four weeks, and though she hadn't suspected any foul play, she knew Judas. One more week, and he'd be back to his old ways. When Judas crept around, he treated Naomi like a fresh, out of the ass, steaming piece of shit, but they'd dealt with their lowest times professionally and Judas had proved to be a brand new man. "Turn around for me." Judas whispered, distracting Naomi from her thoughts. She did as she was told, and was about to straddle Judas when she was interrupted by a faint knock at the door. It got louder, startling them both. Judas shot up from the bed whilst Naomi covered her nakedness with her robe. "It's me, can I come in?" Sydney half cracked the door and poked her head through. "What is it?" Naomi shouted frustrated. It was so typical for Sydney to interrupt a quiet moment between Judas and herself. "Can I come in?" Sydney asked again, opening the door wider and stepping foot into the room. "What Syd? Damn!" Naomi sucked her teeth. Sydney's lack of respect always went unnoticed by Judas. He'd turned into a big kid the moment she'd introduced the two, and they'd spent endless amounts of time together getting acquainted and goofing around. Yet, Sydney had declined any efforts Naomi had made to mend their own relationship from its past breakdown. "You know what, fuck it." Sydney slammed the bedroom door shut and took off out the apartment. She was heated that Judas hadn't returned any of her messages, but what was actually playing on her mind was what was going on between him and Naomi behind their closed bedroom door. She'd intentionally passed their bedroom door on her way out and thought up an excuse to peer inside. She wanted to make sure Judas was good on his word when he'd told her he and Naomi were no longer sexually involved. "See, this is the kind of shit I'm talking about Judas," Naomi said, now in a funk as she stormed to the other side of the room and locked the bedroom door. "Exactly what are you talking about?" Judas asked as picked up on her mood. He knew Sydney's game, and had to give her props for being brave enough to handle her business. What he didn't get, was why Naomi had to blow every situation out of hand. He watched Naomi become emotional while he awaited her reply. "It's just... everything's getting to be too much. The restaurant, Queens, Sydney, and the plans for the wedding... " She fought back her tears. "I feel like Sydney see's you more than I do, your mum see's you more than I do, and she only sees you on a Sunday afternoon." "Awww, Nay. That's what's upsetting you? Shit, I thought you were gonna say you were pregnant, but I hear you." Judas reached out and pulled Naomi into his arms. He held her tight, running his fingers through her short hair and kissing her forehead while she found comfort being pressed against his chest. Sure Judas was crazy about Naomi, but if he wasn't about to play house with Stitches or his other baby mothers then he sure as hell wasn't about to go down that road with her. It was the lack of attention she showed to his private ventures that had attracted him to her initially. She'd deposit money into their business accounts on his request and never question the large withdrawals that accrued twice a week. Judas had no intentions of trading in the game for a white picket fence and a dog named Foyle, but he had known for some time that Naomi didn't feel the same. Don't get it twisted, Naomi was fully aware that her fiancée's success came from poisoning the veins of the weak. As sole distributor of his district, Judas used their businesses to launder his money, securing it safely in a joint account that belonged to himself and his future wife. But, it was times like these when Judas questioned his father's recommendations where his relationship with Naomi was concerned. He'd often reached out to him during their difficult times, and no matter the situation Sensi's response remained the same, "She's the one Judas, trust me." But Judas was beginning to feel unsure. Naomi may have been the woman of his dreams then, but his heart lived in reality and in reality Sydney was his kind of girl!

Chapter 8

"**S**yd, you're something else. I can't believe you had me drive all the way across town to smoke a flipping spliff!" Shelly joked, sticking her head out her driver side window as Sydney crossed the road and got into her Bogie green Nissan Micra. "What's popping?" She asked, with both her bare feet resting on the dashboard. She'd parked three blocks down from Judas and Naomi's apartment as the two had intended on puffing through the night whilst venting about the complex situations they each faced in life. "Let me hit that first," Sydney said, getting in and shutting the door. She knew it wasn't going to be comfortable living under the same roof as her man's woman, especially seeing as his woman was related to her by blood. The announcement of their engagement was the happiest Sydney had seen Naomi since their father's death, but even the guilt she was burdened with in her heart wouldn't let her leave Judas alone. Something inside her willed her to be with him, even when she pulled away. She had no control over his love. "I need to get my own place Shell, Naomi is driving me nuts." Sydney blew smoke and got comfortable in her seat. She rested her head on the head rest and closed her eyes as the herbs went to work on her mind. Sydney was frustrated and confused, torn between the two people she loved more than anything in the world. "Um, hmm, and then what? You do know, Mr. Lover-Boy up there ain't never gonna leave your sister right?" Shelly said breaking Sydney's thoughts of Judas and the love they'd just shared. "This is the type of situation that ends in tears Syd. You think Judas' gonna choose you over twelve years of love?" she asked, continuing their conversation from that afternoon. Sydney shifted in her seat, eyes still closed as she shrugged her shoulders. "I don't know," She replied. She placed the joint between her lips and inhaled once more before passing it back to Shelly, who coughed after her first puff. "See that's why you should mind your own business. It'll teach you to breathe out of that nosey nose of yours," Sydney joked, patting Shelly on the back. "Fuck all that nosey talk Sydney. I'm looking out for you!" Shelly protested whilst catching her breath. "Well I don't need looking out for. And, this is exactly why I didn't want Brittany in my business, I knew she was gonna throw salt in my shit, and have you on her side." Sydney pushed her lips into a pout. "Look Syd, if you want me to stay out of your business, cool." Shelly coughed. "But I ain't gonna pretend that I'm comfortable with this thing between you and Judas. You've only been back a few months and already things are messed up between you and Nay." "Things have always been messed up between me and Naomi, don't act like its news to you," Sydney turned to see if Shelly was for real. "I can't help that I've fallen in love, and neither can he, so just drop it," she concluded trying to avoid a dead end. "Alright, I'll drop it." Shelly sarcastically said, her voice going up a level. "But don't come running to me when you catch Judas butt naked in his own apartment, fucking his future wife," she laughed. "Fuck you Shelly; you're an ass-hole sometimes," Sydney said in amusement. "Judas doesn't even get down like that, trust me!" She alleged. "Well still, I'd rather be an ass-hole than a man-thief," Shelly teased, and then flinched when Sydney playfully slapped her thigh. "You ain't got any morals, have you? On a level, it's like he's playing you both," she concluded before passing the spliff back Sydney's way. "Shell shut up!" Sydney shouted, cutting her eye, and inhaling the herbs. "Naomi and Judas were going through a dry spell way before I was on the scene." "And I suppose you're just helping out right?" Shelly said, laughing harder, intoxicated from her high. Sydney contemplated slapping Shelly, but she blamed her arrogance on their high. "Seriously Shell, I'm feeling this Nigga, he's paid and swinging," Sydney teased. "He's got me hooked differently. He looks at me and my knees go under, he touches me, and I shudder, and when he kisses me it's all over." Shelly sighed as if in her own world. "He put it on me differently this evening, we were kissing and stripping all at once when Judas' crazy ass lifts me against the breakfast bar, balances me there, and pushes his dick in me without so much as a heads up. I don't even remember what happened to my draws." Sydney shuddered from the memory. "Okay, so he's got skills, but I hoped you used a condom," Shelly said turning up her nose. "I stand my ground when I say Judas is a hoe." "Yeah we used a rubber, the man has nine inches of goodness, but I ain't getting ready to die for it," Sydney replied, glad to see Shelly had begun rolling another joint. All this negativity was messing up her high. "Nine inches, fuck off." Shelly screamed almost knocking over the weed and tobacco she'd separated onto a CD cover she'd found in her car. She thought about all the times Bradley viciously rammed his penis inside her and tried to recall his length, but her thoughts were soon replaced with a sickness in her stomach, so she quickly regained her composure and said, "He can't be nine inches, can he?" "About nineish," Sydney replied unaware of her close friends shock at his size. "My body can't help but stiffen from pleasure when he enters me, and with every stroke he gives me, my body yearns for more." Shelly licked the sticky side of the Rizla paper, wide eyed, eating the words out of Sydney's mouth. She hated the entire male race, including her own father for his neglect during her abuse. Because of this, she believed no man could make a woman feel that good, especially a monster like Judas. He didn't fool Shelly; she'd been around men like him all her life. They used people and manipulated them into making choices that they wouldn't have made had they not been an addict for that thing called love. Behind closed eyes, Sydney listened to the rain as it began to beat on the roof of Shelly's car, and drifted back to the moment she dug her neatly manicured fingers into the small of Judas's back whilst he penetrated her beyond her years of pleasure. The beating of her heart had soon returned her attention to the pulsating warmth she still had between her legs, reminding her that her lover was there. "I love you Sydney." She remembered Judas saying as the breakfast bar shook, and he climaxed, both of them sticky and out of breath. Sydney lay back and shuddered, satisfied and exhausted. She didn't care if they never cuddled after sex, and did the whole pillow talk thing. Her baby loved her, and that was all she needed to know. She'd made up her mind then, that she would make him hers, even if it killed her.

Chapter 9

Just minutes before mid-night, when the inmates and prison officers had begun to settle down for a long night, Nathan Jacobs climbed down from the top bunk of the bunk bed he shared with his bucktooth cellmate. He pulled a loose brick out of the wall and retrieved a slim Nokia 8210 mobile phone he'd hustled it out of another inmate earlier that day. He knew if his cellmate had gotten his hands on the phone his future plans would have been ruined. He switched on the device, and watched it load, then dialed out, waiting for the line on the other end to connect. "Cuz!" Nathan whispered into the receiver, being careful not to wake his cellmate who had recently begun to fill the cell with snores. "Who's this?" The receiver of the call replied out of breath. Nathan could hear the sounds of pots and plates being handled in the background behind his cousin's voice, and presumed he was either at home, or in a kitchen of some sort. Either way it seemed safe for them to talk. "It's me Cuz, Nathan!" Nathan said, pacing the confined cell as he spoke. He hadn't called his cousin for a chit-chat or a reunion, his call was personal. Nathan knew that the information he held would be beneficial to both him and his older cousin in the near future, providing he survived his current sentence. "Nathan! What's up? Where you staying at and why you whispering Cuz?" Nathan's cousin replied, firing a handful of questions at once. Nathan hadn't yet called his parents and informed them that he had been picked up by the police, nor had he contacted his pregnant girlfriend and informed her that he wouldn't be attending the birth of their first child. He was sure they'd start to question his whereabouts, and his cousin Cee was now his last hope. "I got shafted man!" Nathan confessed. "I was stupid to trust this dude I met in East. Man had me, Felt, and Tennyson hyped to join his team. We were down for making money with him, and putting in work but the fucker jerked us off, and for what?" He rambled, making no sense to his older cousin who had slipped away from his current distraction to give his younger cousin his full attention. "Sounds like you got yourself a situation. What you need, cash or a solicitor?" Cee replied. He was determined to do whatever it took to put his baby cousin at ease. It was Nathan's first time in the pen, so it was natural for him to freak out the way he was, but what Cee didn't get was why he was reaching out to him. Nathan's father was a straight dog in his youth, and Nathan was his seventh son. Still, Cee listened intensely as Nathan broke down to him what had gone down the previous week, and soon became intrigued by the knowledge his younger cousin had obtained during the short amount of time he'd spent on his side of town. Cee ended his conversation with his cousin by instructing him to sit tight, and remain calm. He promised

Nathan he'd put a healthy amount of money on his books by morning, and that he'd see if he had any connects in the pen that had any information on the whereabouts of his boys Tennyson and Felt. He winced, and held his hand out as instructed by the beautiful woman who'd cleaned his wound and stitched him up after he'd been grazed by a bullet during a robbery at his home the previous week. He'd heard rumors of his connect robbing clientele for their product just hours after they'd made the transition between product and cash. The thought of purposely being made a fool had brought Cee's blood to a boil. He remembered the last time he was hit up for his product. He'd been left with no option but to crawl back to his connect with his tail between his legs, dragging himself deeper into the game. "Shit, that fucking hurts!" Cee hollered, when the woman attending to his wound applied a solution to stop the infection before re-bandaging up his arm. "Doesn't everything?" she replied, setting him straight. She knew all too well of the kinds of antic's that brought thugs like Cee to her home. She cleaned him up in record time and insisted on walking him to the door. The only real reason she'd worked on him that night was because he'd promised to pay her double services, and he was cute. Thanks to her daughter's father and a long list of his friends, she knew everything in the hood had a price, but whether it was all worth paying for, she wasn't so sure.

Chapter 10

Samantha Clarke pushed her set of keys into the salon door and placed her purse in the opening, leaving it ajar whilst she returned to her car. She was out of breath and already perspiring, yet just as she'd opened the car boot, the shop phone began to ring, leaving her little time to close and secure her car in an attempt to catch the call. "Good morning, this is Queens. How can I help?" Samantha sang down the phone, out of breath, but in her usual morning voice. "Oh, hey Sam, is Naomi there?" asked Mariah, one of Naomi's hairstylists whilst loudly chewing on a piece of gum. "No Mariah, its Monday." Samantha checked the time on her watch, and took a deep breath. Monday mornings or 'Murder Monday', as Samantha called it, was Naomi's deposit day and one of the busiest days of the week. "Well I'm gonna be a little late, can you let her know for me?" Mariah asked, unconcerned how her absence would affect the rest of the staff. Samantha never questioned Naomi's reasoning for hiring such an irresponsible, disorganized, and inefficient hairstylist, but she couldn't wait to see her fired. She didn't have time to speak her mind to Mariah, as the alarm on her car drew her attention away from the phone. "Its fine Mariah, I'll tell Naomi when she gets here." She rushed the call, before placing the phone on the receiver and racing out to her car. She slowed her pace when she recognized the face of the young, handsome boy disarming her car alarm. Then she mentally scolded herself for leaving the key in the ignition. She'd had a lot on her mind lately, what with her husband's imprisonment, and her twin boy's quickly turning into men. "Isn't it enough that I have to deal with their antics at home?" she muttered to herself, as she stood with her hands on her hips at the salon door. The eldest of her twins, Kieran, paced towards her with his backpack on his shoulders in a hunch, and clutching his jacket to shield himself from the cold. "Why the hell aren't you at school Kieran?" she snapped, holding out her hand for her keys. Kieran dropped the keys into his mother's open hand, then walked right past her into the salon, and threw himself into an empty chair. "What's up Sam?" said Stacey, another stylist on his way in. He nodded at Kieran who nodded back, then went about his business of setting up his station. Yet, he was listening; ears wide open, with his back to the two as they deliberated the situation they'd found themselves in. "Boy, you better have a damned good excuse as to why you ain't at school this morning," Samantha spoke to her son with clout, "Do you know how much I spend on you and your brother's uniforms? Way too much for the both of you to be walking around in the streets with it on for fun. What did they send you home for this time Kieran?" She asked, her voice getting louder. "Fighting? What?" Samantha screeched at the top of her lungs. Kieran didn't reply. He knew whatever he said would only rile his mother up more, so he let her frustration go over his head and stayed sulking in his chair. It wasn't like him to be rebellious and hostile, but lately he'd been acting up which was more his brother's style. Like his brother Kareem, Kieran was thick bodied, and built strong like their father. Kieran had long braids that stopped almost at the middle of his back while Kareem had been rocking a low fade for the last two years. Inseparable from birth, and uncannily the same, Kieran and Kareem were vastly approaching fifteen and already stood at 5'9, towering over all the boys in their year. Samantha didn't have time to argue with Kieran at such an early hour in the morning. She shook her head at her son's stubbornness, and began to make her way to her station when she noticed a group of young thugs on the other side of the street looking directly at her, beating their fists into their hands and snarling. Samantha looked over at Kieran who had shot up from his chair with both his hands balled into tight fists. "Sit down!" she hissed through gritted teeth as Kieran heaved with a look of revenge plastered on his face. The teenagers made gestures with their hands that Samantha couldn't understand, but Kieran knew what they meant. They were looking past her at him, and he seemed to understand what their gestures meant very well.

Chapter 11

Judas stood pressed against his parked car on a side street off Old Street, and waited impatiently. He had already smoked near half a joint and contemplated rolling another when he spotted one of his girls emerged from the block across the street. The twenty-something year old woman strutted her stuff, and hugged her light brown fur coat, swaying her hips Judas's way. Judas licked his lips and flicked the ash of his joint before taking one last puff and putting it out. The sexy female approached him with much attitude, and then stopped. With both her hands on her hips and an unimpressed look on her face, she let Judas know she was vexed. "What's good Mariah?" asked Judas in a sexy boyish tone as he blew smoke. He loved it when Mariah was mad at him, though it took some time to wear her down. Mariah was stubborn beyond belief, but all her frustrations could be worked out at a price. "Evidently not me," Mariah shot, whilst chewing on a piece of gum and snapping her neck. "Am I not worth a phone call Judas, a fucking text at least?" She raved with her hands dancing in the air. Judas had to admit that Mariah looked mouth-watering in her brown fur Moschino jacket with the leather stripes around the waist. It complemented her skin-tight, French Connection jeans and her all black knee-high Ugg boots. Mariah's untimely cooperation and her ability to keep her mouth shut earned her a spot in Judas's corrupt team. While not the brightest chick on the block, Mariah was a born grafter and put in good work. Judas knew he needn't waste his time bickering with the girl on the street corner. He turned around, opened his car door, reached in and pulled a thin, light green box out of his glove compartment. Mariah's expression suddenly changed. "What you got in there?" she asked as her eyes lit up. "You want this huh?" Judas smiled, teasing Mariah with the box. Initially he'd purchased the £3,565 Tiffany and Co charm bracelet for Naomi, but she hadn't been acting herself lately. Plus, the last thing he wanted was for her to suspect that he and Sydney were messing around under her nose, but since he was in the clear he could put the bracelet to better use. Judas smiled, pleased with the new expression on Mariah's face. He held his hand out for her to accept, and watched her silently admire the white gold Tiffany & Co charm bracelet whilst he attached it around her wrist. "See, I knew you weren't mad at me." Judas whispered in Mariah's ear once he'd pulled her close, and had his arms secured around her waist. Mariah stood, wearing a stupid grin. She was still taken back by the diamonds on the piece, not to mention the weight it put on her arm. Judas had bought her a shit load of expensive, designer items, but nothing came close to this. "Nah, I'm not mad Judas, I just missed you," she said, softening her tone. She became putty in his arms, but she wasn't letting him off that easy. The Millions cologne he wore by Paco Rabanne drove her senses crazy, but she cleared her throat and composed herself before disengaging herself from his grasp. 'Damn I love this boy!' She thought to herself as she turned and lead the way to her flat. The two bedroom flat on the fourth floor that Mariah rented on Bowma Road in Old Street was fully financed, and maintained by Judas himself. It was his fiancée Naomi who Mariah had first made acquaintance with at the Black & Beautiful Hair Show. It was there Naomi saw her do her thing. Shortcuts were Mariah's specialty, and seeing as Naomi was on a quest to find a new stylist amongst the conventions contenders, Mariah had made it a point to see that her models hair caught every attending salon owner's eye. Fortunately, she hadn't noticed Judas standing next to Naomi during their discussion, or it would have been on from day one, because for once Mariah was more interested in the opportunity presented to her when Naomi complimented her work, and said she would be willing to double her client list and whatever her former employer was paying her if she could start the following weekend. Naomi's timing couldn't have been more on point. Mariah had been sleeping on her girlfriend Casey's sofa. Being unemployed, Mariah had only entered the 'Stylists of the Year' competition as a way to get her name back in the styling industry. Owning her own salon was her biggest dream, but without a space and the funds to work with, Mariah was running short of options on which she could depend. At first Casey was cool with Mariah's customers coming through her place to get their hair done.

As long as Mariah helped out with the utility bills and kept her shit tight for free, Casey was game. She already rocked a short cut, so Mariah didn't mind the random request for a re- touch or a shape-up around the back. She even crossed Casey's palm with money for all the hair products, and water she used, yet Casey always found a reason to complain. If it wasn't one thing it was the other. First, it was the wet towels Mariah left lying on the bathroom floor, and then it was the amount of space her black bags were taking up in the lounge, black bags which contained her clothes. Naomi's offer of a job couldn't have come at a better time. In a matter of weeks after Mariah joined the stylists at Queens, her chair was fully booked, and she was- if only a small step, closer to her dream. Biggie Smalls wasn't lying when he spat 'Mo' Money, Mo' Problems!' because for the longest time it was the theme song to Mariah's life. Due to being a Coke addict, Casey lost her job at Selfridges, and decided to use her last pay cheque to feed her habit instead of paying the rent. The landlord came down on them hard. He didn't mind Mariah staying with Casey, they were obedient, clean and quiet tenants, but as it turned out Casey had stopped paying the rent months before Mariah had started out at Queens. It was like a hard slap in the face. Casey had been charging Mariah 'Rent,' and instead of her paying shit like she was supposed to, she'd been using it to satisfy her need for a substance that ate away at the tissue in her nose. "It's really fucked up the situation you girls get yourselves into. I feel for you, I really do, but Naomi would kill me if she knew I let the both of you spend the night here. This ain't a hostel, it's a place of work Mariah, you know that!" Judas had said firmly when he'd found Casey trying to talk Mariah out of crying her eyes out in the staff locker rooms at the end of her shift at Queens. It was closing time on a Friday night in June, and Naomi and Samantha had left out early to hit a club, something they rarely did, leaving Judas to count the days earnings and lock up for the night. Coincidentally, it was the same night that Mariah had said 'fuck you' to another night in a public toilet and had taken the risk of laying low in the locker room in Queens for a few nights until she could figure out her next move. "Look, you don't have to tell Naomi!" Mariah had jumped up and grabbed Judas arm in an attempt to save herself any more embarrassment in her state. "We'll be gone by the morning. She won't even know we're here, I promise. Just let us stay for one night? We don't have anywhere else to go." Mariah had pleaded through tears that eventually melted Judas' heart. He was adamant, and kept his word when he said Mariah and Casey couldn't spend the night in Queens. He wasn't stupid enough to leave a crack-head, and her desperate girlfriend alone in his fiancée's pride and joy, but he'd had a better idea. One that would be useful for all of them. "Yo Judas, what's up man? You got a minute?" shouted Chad, a loyal informative customer and tenant from the top floor, out of his window, as Mariah and Judas approached the entrance of the block. "Hold up man, I'll be right with you." Judas shouted up. "Keep your scary ass in your flat." He chuckled, as did Mariah, when the both of them were secured inside the building, and had begun to make their way up the eight flights of stairs to the fourth floor. "When you gonna go up there and see what he wants?" Mariah asked while she searched her purse for the gate key. "You know his babymums' gonna stay on his ass about the damn smell that keeps creeping into their flat, right?" she pressed. The fourth floor, where Mariah's flat was situated at the end on the right of the balcony, was secured by a large steel gate. Her front door was also gated, and double locked from the inside out. "Fuck Chad and his babymum!" Judas replied snatching the small bunch of keys out of Mariah's hand. "If they can't deal with the smell, they can move the fuck out," he said, loud enough for his tenants to hear as he unlocked the first gate and proceeded to unlock the next. "I'm just saying Judas, its nigga's like Chad who's complaining and shit's gonna be our fall. His loud mouth's gonna end up bringing all us fuckers down." Mariah said while tapping the door in a way that only Casey recognized and understood. "Mariah! I thought you were due in at Queens?" Casey said excitedly opening the door on the chain and peering through the crack. She was still cautious even though Mariah had used their secret knock, but upon seeing Mariah, her best friend pulled the door closed, removed the chain and opened the door just enough for Mariah to come inside. "Get outta the fucking way you clown," Judas spat when Casey accidentally pushed the door on him, unaware that Judas was also standing on the other side. "Oh my God, I'm so sorry Judas. Mariah, tell him I'm sorry! Damn girl, where'd you get that? Let me see, come over here." Casey rambled about almost crazy like, and then immediately directed her attention and eyes on the bright item dangling from Mariah's right arm. "Take your ass back over there and get back to work." Judas grabbed Casey by her bare arm and pulled her away from Mariah, sending her reeling into the work-room. Casey stumbled awkwardly into the door frame, slightly hitting her head. None of the naked women looked up from their work, but they all became quite upon Judas's arrival. "Damn Judas, why do you have to man handle Casey like that?" Mariah rushed to Casey's aid and picked her up from the floor. Judas entered the work room with an attitude, and glared at the nakedness of the dozen women standing over the long, oddly placed tables. "Don't worry about him Case, he's just mad because he's gotta go see 'Stinky Chad' before his needle sticking ass stops paying his rent," Mariah whispered, squeezing Casey's shoulder before stripping out of her clothes. The working women kept their heads down. They all stood around a long table piling ounces of pure white cocaine, which was constantly being produced and brought in by trolley from the kitchen by 'Cook,' ready to be diced-up and wrapped in Clingfilm, so Judas and his team could distribute to their dealers on the streets by the kilo. "Sticks, is that you?" asked Judas, answering his phone and walking out the work room into the small smoke filled kitchen situated on the left. The women wasted no time loosening up, and getting their talk on, admiring Mariah's new gift. Mariah watched him take his call. "Is this just a fly and visit, or are you here to roll up your sleeves and put in some work?" The oldest of the women remaining at the table snarled, only turning to get a glimpse at the bracelet that had all the other women in the room hovering over Mariah in awe. "Of course, she's staying, ain't you Mariah?" Casey asked rubbing the small bump that had risen up in the middle of her forehead. "Nah Case, I gotta be back at Queens by this afternoon." Mariah replied half recognizing her childhood friend. In the two years Mariah and Casey had been residing in Bowma Towers, Mariah had been able to hold down a job whilst Casey was lucky if she held down a day's meal. Casey was frail and severely underweight. Mariah looked at her friend with pitying eyes. She looked at the bracelet on her wrist, and then back to her friend. "You ladies better get back to work before Judas brings his ass back in here!" She said grabbing Casey's hand and pulling her through the work room into the large room situated at the back that served as their living quarters. Everyone in the work-house knew Mariah and Judas were creeping around, yet Mariah continued to play their relationship off as rumors and nothing else. She couldn't have cared less about the snide remarks she got from the other women outside her door. They worked on her property, for her man Judas, the son of Sensi AKA Detective Mendez. "I don't know how you do it Mariah!" Casey shook her raggedy head as she sat sprawled out naked on her single bed. "You're fucking the two most notorious and powerful men in the town and have em both eating out the palm of your hand," she continued, a little louder than Mariah would have liked. "Tell the whole world why you don't!" Mariah placed a finger to her mouth signaling for Casey to lower her voice. "I ain't ready for this to end yet, I still got plans for Mr. Mendez. And besides..." Mariah glanced down at her bracelet once more. "I'm in love with his son. I know you think I'm crazy Casey, but I'm not. Judas and

I are meant to be together. Maybe not now or even next year, but it's coming I can tell. Whatever it is he's got up his sleeve, I want my share. I refuse to walk away without what's been promised to me." Mariah stood up and admired her naked body with all its curves. "You think I don't know what's happening Mariah? You haven't fallen in love with him, you're in love with the game. You've fallen in love with the idea of you and Judas." Casey rolled over on her mattress and laughed a toothless laugh, comfortable in her naked state. "You must be crazy if you think Judas is gonna one day up and leave his prissy wife for some dope baking twenty-nine year old nothing from the hood." Casey was confident in her own room and spoke her mind like she often would when none of the other females were about. She never left the flat like Mariah did every day for work. She ate, worked, slept and shat within the four walls of 108 Bowma Tower and had seen many women like Mariah come and go. She dumbed herself down around Judas, and the females in the work rooms, thus earning her the opportunity to learn a thing or two. For one, Judas's team played by the barter rule: 'You do something for me, and I'll do something for you.' Except the only thing they ever wanted in return for a favor was your silence. For example, Mariah's sparkling gift. Judas was taking an enormous risk accommodating his side piece while she worked for his future wife. He gave Mariah material things to secure her loyalty and silence of their affair. He never gave her enough to leave because she had shown him the limits he'd need to go in order for her to stay. Casey had never met Judas's fiancée Naomi, but before her addiction, she'd seen her around the way, and heard enough about her from Mariah to know who she was. Naomi never came by the work house. In fact, Mariah was almost sure she didn't know that it existed. But Casey knew better. Women like Naomi never questioned their men regarding their conduct on the streets. Naomi had her sources, who'd eventually notify her of vital information when the time was right. She was in her position by right, the Queen in Judas's game, and Mariah was a mare pawn. Casey sat up, and watched as Mariah re-applied her make-up and touched up her hair. If there were ever a time when she needed to start putting money away, it was now. Maybe she'd ask Essen for a raise. She thought of different scenarios in which Judas and Mariah got caught, them playing out in her head. There was only one way that Judas and Mariah's affair was going to end and that was in a mixture of violence and tears, Judas was never going to leave Naomi for Mariah. Casey could bet that on her life.

Chapter 12

amien Fenton, AKA Sticks, switched on his IPhone and dialed the number of the only friend who'd had his back while he was locked down. "What's good fam?" Sticks asked in a thuggish tone when the line had been connected. "You tell me player?" Judas replied with the same depth in his voice. Both he and Sticks had attended Weatherhigh Primary School, and their relationship went way beyond the block. For Judas, not having Sticks around was like missing a finger, his trigger finger. Sticks was commonly described as a rich golden brown brother, around 5ft8, with thick eye-lashes, rocking a slight high-top. He walked out of the institute wearing a white wife-beater, and a dark blue pair of Levi jeans, minus his usual diamond and platinum encrusted jewelry. He was naked. "Where the hell are you man?" Sticks asked arrogantly down the phone. "I know your dad's filled you in about my release." He was thrilled to be a free man. Judas could only shake his head and wonder how his father managed to bend the rules of the law yet again. Sticks was the kind of man who'd shoot first and ask questions later. He was honest and loyal to his own, but his dirty fetish for young girls left him with a string of unspent convictions due to the lack of cooperation his victims gave in court. Sticks often found himself moving from place to place, preying on females in different towns and districts as his own had labeled him somewhat of a sexual beast. It was for that nature which Sticks had been incarcerated. He'd been caught messing around with a ripened fifteen year old from Brixton. Kenosha was beside herself, fucking with what her and her little school friends would call 'a real nigga'. He had the young girl skip school on his request, while they spent countless hours getting high and having rough sex. It was in that state that her father, Principal Perkins had found her, and manipulated her into calling the embarrassing situation rape. Judas's hesitance told Sticks that he knew nothing of his release. Still, he walked out the prison with his head held high, ignoring the watchful eyes of the prison guards as he left the premises. With the steel gate now secured behind him, he was pleased that the situation he'd taken care of had effectively met the demands that Sensi had made in return for his release. "You know, I heard about that bit of trouble you had with them youngsters you recruited from South." Sticks said testing Judas's knowledge of his father's future plans. "You heard about that yeah?" Judas asked oblivious to how Sticks could have obtained such information whilst he was behind the wall. But Sticks thought it was strange that Judas hadn't asked how he'd made bail. That was the least on his mind though, as he just hoped Sensi was a man of his word, and all charges on his case were dropped like they'd agreed. "Please tell me that wasn't Sticks you were just talking to and that I didn't just hear you say he's been released?" Cook turned from her stove with a wooden spoon in one hand, the other on her waist, and a white mask covering the lower part of her face. "I thought that was his third strike. Who'd he kill to get out?" Cook questioned as Essen entered the kitchen and pounded Judas, fist to fist, as he stood on the other side of Cook watching her work the stove. "Who's being released?" Essen asked attempting to catch up on the conversation he'd missed. He pulled a chair out from under the table and sat down. Judas followed and did the same. "Sticks is coming home." Cook replied through her mask, not once taking her eyes off the stove. "Can you believe the nigga phoned me just now, talking about he thought my dad told me he was being released and that one of us was picking him up." Judas said annoyed. "Well I know he ain't waiting on my ass to pick him up." Essen responded in disgust. He despised Sticks' disposition towards young women and girls, and thought that prison was the best place for people like him. He'd seen Sticks in action around vulnerable females, and wanted to kill him himself. Essen was livid though he never showed it. He couldn't believe that Sensi had had him play a role in a plan that involved putting a vulture like Sticks back on the streets. "I don't know what the hell my dad was thinking? I mean I love Sticks that's my boy, don't get me wrong. But we can't keep beefing theses dope boys from outta town because our homeboy can't keep his nasty hands to himself." "Or his dick in his pants," Jada added, as Judas continued to curse his father's dictation of how he ran his team. Every Lick Sensi put Judas up on presented a different environment for his people to walk into and get killed. Before Sticks' arrest, he was in charge of what Judas liked to call 'Collections'. But since then, his photograph had been plastered all over the TV. Despite his sexually explicit behavior, Sticks was the only person on the team that was undoubtedly crude and sly. He'd hit four men for their product already, right after they'd collected it from him themselves. There wasn't a doubt in Judas's mind that Sticks could pull off the next lick, but because of his exposure Sticks had to lay low. It had been almost two weeks, since Judas had set three naive young hustlers onto his last victim. And because of a miscommunication in the information they were all currently sitting in jail. Sensi was well aware of the pressures Judas was currently dealing with, being that he was constantly losing members of his team. But the Detective didn't care. All he cared about was the financial freedom he got at his son's expense. Ever since, Sensi had been promoted to Detective, Judas had had the rush sucked out of the game. Sensi was always getting in there before he got a chance to enjoy the chase, which was ironic because growing up, Judas remembered how being in the game used to feel. Judas knew his father to be one of Hackney's 'Top Dogs'. 'Hustle', was what they called Sensi in the streets. And he lived up to the name like there was no other means. In his younger days, Sensi was a straight up Thug, the suits he wore now, replacing his street swag made him look stupid to anyone who knew him then, and much older that he actually was. He still had two gold teeth in his mouth, replacing his incisors', and he kept his hair lined up straight even with his new strands of grey. "As soon as you step out onto that board with intent son, there's no turning back. You roll the dice a few times, you win, as long as you don't cheat then the game gone treat you good, but you gots to keep moving to play, There's always gonna be a much faster, and younger player, right behind you waiting to take your spot. If another player gets in your way, take em out. It's an open board son, ain't nowhere to hide, and there ain't nowhere to run." "In this game, you're standing at the gates of heaven, with hell breathing fire at your back. You can't afford to come in second place, cos second place is a watered-down word for 'motherfucker you lost'. Don't get comfortable in another players game son, be smart. Cos if hells riding on his ass and you behind him, then my friend, you're already dead." Those were Sensi's own words. He told his son, 'No matter what, you can't get out the game and be straight.' So how'd he do it? He used his own son as a pawn that's how. Nobody had any real respect for Judas on the streets, what they had was fear, and their fear was for the law, the law being his old man. Judas distributed cocaine by the kilo, to hustlers, too scared to get caught buying anywhere else. He was the face of his father's criminal activity yet his reputation was weak. Taxing his customers just wasn't enough, it wasn't the money that Judas loved about the game it was the fame, he saw hustlers below him every day, switching cars, draped in diamonds, showcasing the work they'd put in on the roads. For Sensi's sake Judas and his team were made to invest. Hustling was in his nature, but, in fact, it wasn't worth doing if he couldn't enjoy the fruit of his labor. He felt stuck in his god forsaken hood, with no outlet to his desires. Sensi had one thing right. 'If a players gets in your way, take em out' . Judas had been caught up in his father's antics for some time now and it was getting to that time when a nigga had to start a game of his own. Yeah, Judas respected his father as a solder, but real hustlers don't play with cops. Sensi would have to find some other prick to do his dirty work when Judas got the call he'd been waiting for from his soon to be business partner; Lock. "I got another job from my dad lined up for tonight." Judas lifted his head off the table and said. Both Essen and Cook looked at him, with raised eyebrows. Neither of them said a word. They didn't have to. "Don't worry; I didn't expect either of you two to jump on it." Judas snarled disappointed that neither of the two even played with the thought of putting themselves out for the team. Taking parts in robberies was child's play for Essen, this Judas knew. Essen could easily walk into a room, shoot a motherfucker in the face, wipe his tool clean, and walk out like he hadn't just committed a crime. And Cook, she wasn't you average hood-chick, she was, and always had been 100% down for the cause. She grew up with her Spanish family on Amhurst Road, and because of her pretty looks she learnt fast, how to cut the local bitches up with her just her tongue. Either of them could have taken the job, but even Judas knew it wasn't worth the risk. Cook cooked Crack like it was an old family recipe, and nobody could replace a guy like Essen on Judas's team. It just couldn't be done. "Look, I'm calling a meeting tonight. Tell Spades, Trina and Nugget they all need to be there. If worst comes to worst, we're all rolling through the West End like in the old school." Judas pounded Essen as he got up from around the table to leave. Today's meeting would be to welcome Sticks home, though it wasn't actually needed, Judas knew that no one on his team was that trusting of his father security, especially after what had happened to the last Collectors who had taken the last job, but it was still early in the day. Hackney was home to many impressible characters. There was always some unloved soul dressed as a thug hanging outside Queens hoping to get recognized and recruited into Judas's team.

Chapter 13

When Naomi walked into Queens, she was a Queen in her own domain. Before she could read she was styling hair, and when she could read she was reading about, styling hair. It was almost overwhelming walking through the large double glass doors and seeing her face or cut on the front cover of some of those exact magazines she read when she was a child, blown up and hung on her walls. Judas had hired the best of the best interior designers in London to create a feeling of elegance, and class with just a dash of culture in the heart of the hood. Proudly Naomi entered her place of business with a contented glow. It was marvelous to see all her employees hard at work. That was all except for one. She climbed the nine large white steps that led to upper level of the Salon where her office was situated on the left, and her beauticians worked their magic on an ever growing list of customers to the right. "What happened to you last night Nay? I thought you said you were gonna call me back?" Samantha, Naomi's best friend and sidekick stood by the door of her office and asked about a half an hour after Naomi had come in to start her day. Naomi sat herself behind her solid oak wooden desk profoundly pounding numbers into a calculator. She sat dumbfounded; as she couldn't understand the figures on the statement the bank teller had produced her with that morning. They didn't match up to the figures she had in her log book, in the Salon. According to the statement Naomi got from the bank the balance in her business account was just short of a Mill with deposits being made almost every day. Naomi didn't even notice Samantha watching her frustrate over the figures she'd begun repeatedly scribbling down. Her mind was set on proving the bank teller wrong, or at least make sense of what she believed to be a mistake. "Is everything alright?" Samantha asked. Still Naomi didn't respond until she had calculated the difference and was sure her own figures were correct. "Sorry Sam, hey what's up?" Was her delayed reaction, followed by a deep breath. "What's up with Kieran, is he sick?" She asked. She remembered seeing one of Samantha's son's slumped in one of the chairs on the ground floor. "Ahh no, Mr. Clark and I have some things to talk about when we get home." Samantha stretched her head to the side to get a quick peek of her son. "I just don't understand boys." She shook her head and said rolling her eyes. "Yeah well try understanding men." Naomi replied getting up from her desk, and walking to towards Samantha on the landing. Both women looked, over the banister of the first floor onto the busy salon below them and sighed. Samantha had put as must effort and work into the establishment as Naomi had done financially, and together they'd relinquished their childhood dream. "You know I ask for one thing Sam. One thing for myself and he taints it." Naomi complained to her girl. "Taint's what?" Samantha questioned. She knew Naomi was speaking in code. It was classic Naomi Henderson, Hackney's own ghetto queen to get all uppity and snobbish now that she had moved up, and out of the hood. "I requested a statement from the bank today, and the balance figure they gave me doesn't match the figure's I've logged in the books. I mean I had no idea that any deposits or withdrawals besides the ones I made were being made on the account. What was Judas thinking? I could have been arrested for fraud." Naomi whispered amongst the chatter in the salon, careful not to mention her current balance in the account. "Don't tell me Judas is cleaning it out!" Samantha said fretful, she never did trust Judas even if her own husband and best friend deemed him trustworthy and loyal. "Samantha, don't be stupid!" Naomi laughed at the thought of Judas cleaning out her account. "He's adding to my deposits, I guess washing his shit through my account and my name." "So!" Samantha shrieked, "It's you account ain't it, so it's your money right." She snapped her neck. "No Sam, it's my personal account. Judas has crossed the line. He's got no right to putting drug money up in my shit." Naomi said through the ruckus that Judas himself had created amongst the women downstairs, when he'd entered the establishment followed shortly by Mariah and Essen. "Well you better go handle your business." Samantha said discreetly before descending down the stairs. She greeted Judas and Essen before returning to the floor where Mariah had already slipped behind her station and had began attending to a client whilst gossiping with the crowd. That's just what I'm about to do, Naomi thought as she led the men into her office and shut the door. As well as a the large, oak, desk in the middle of Naomi's office, two large red leather sofa's sat against a pure white wall decorated with a large framed picture of a bright red thorn-less rose. Like her apartment Naomi's office was decorated with elegance and style. When it came to their expensive lifestyle Judas would spare no expense, and of course Naomi was no fool to what he did on the streets. It was practically the talk of the town. She had used what finances she had been able to salvage from her father's fallen empire, and contributed it towards Queens. As a modern-day woman she knew firsthand how imperative it was to have financial independence. Naomi's mother had sold her soul for her fortune, and like the devil, her fortune sold her out, Naomi sat behind her desk, legs crossed and picked up her pen. She wrote down a figure on a post-it note, detached the small square from its pad and passed it to Judas to read. Judas sucked his teeth and screwed the note up in his palm. The last thing he wanted to discuss in front of his boy, and partner, was his current financial state. He wondered sometimes about Naomi's actions and the way she voiced her opinions on the choices he made. She hadn't questioned him when he'd spent near £52,000 a piece on the twin pearl BMW X5's they were driving, nor did she think about the damage she was doing having a financial advisor looking over their accounts. Judas trusted no one who wasn't a part of his team, and made a mental note to reconsider Naomi's authority over their accounts, including the account for Queens. He'd done well with what he'd made from the sale of the shares, and assets he'd sold using her name. With his father's knowledge of law he was able to manipulate Naomi into believing that the bulk of her father's establishments and properties were now owned by the government, he produced paper work, and auction statements stating that they were illegally bought and now remained in police custody until sold at auction or destroyed. "Well?" Naomi said waiting for an explanation. "Well what? It's my business, but we can discuss it later if you want." Judas replied with a distasteful look on his face. His brows winced together, and the base in his voice shock Naomi a little, but her business wasn't some bitch that he was fucking in the streets it was her livelihood, if not her life. She had never felt the need to question the initial net worth of their accounts, she never looked over the accounts of their other businesses, nor did she look over the leases of their Residential Block. Not even to see who lived in it. Naomi made a mental note to investigate all of the above.

Chapter 14

S oaping up her sponge with Imperial Leather soap, Sydney scrubbed away at the stench of cigarettes and alcohol imbedded in her pores from the establishment she'd woken up in at sunrise. She wasn't sore down below which was always a healthy sign, and lucky for her, Naomi and Judas were fast asleep when she put her key in the front door and tip-toed across the hall to her bedroom. She always had the sweetest sleep after an episode, which was fucked up, but kind of rewarding. As other nights she'd fight sleep, for fear of giving in to their demands. Fourteen years ago, when Sydney was just twelve, she was diagnosed with Dissociative Identity Disorder after she blacked out and beat the school nurse senseless, during her first year in HGCH School. At the time, she was already being treated by a family doctor for schizophrenia three times a week. Her father paid for the best treatment available, and she was learning techniques and trying new things that slowed her episodes down. She was able to keep her disorder under medicated control, but then her father was murdered, and all the treatment she received from their family doctor stopped. The government took over her care, labeling her unstable, and partially locking her away. Experience, was her doctor now. Sydney turned the water pressure up on the wall, and pulled the bobby pin out her hair, and closed her eyes. She let the force of the hot water beat down on her skin while the bathroom filled up with steam and the music she was playing in the background faded out. Deborah Cox's –'Nobody's Supposed to be here,' was a long time favorite of hers, but at that moment, whilst ridding her body of mystery's she could only imagine occurred the night before. She celebrated being Sydney. She submitted herself to the waters relaxing sensation for a few minutes longer before squeezing out her hair, and twisting it into a bun. She grabbed a towel off the towel rack and stepped out the bath. Sydney had slept well into the day, and by now Naomi would be holding down the fort at Queens while Judas got up to whatever it was he did on the streets. She didn't have to be a genius to guess that Judas sold drugs. It was all in his swag, and truth be told it was what turned Sydney on. She walked through the apartment in her towel alone, bare footed with her hair wrapped in a wet bun, and was reminded of the first time she'd made a play for her sister's man. Paige, the youngest personality Sydney held caged had been feeling Judas from the moment they'd arrived. Sydney had being held against her will in the Cleverfield Mental Clinic in Northampton, where she was being forced medication for her disorder, and kept under the watchful eyes of the nurses and staff. The last thing Sydney wanted to hear about upon her release was Naomi's fiancée Judas. But that was all Naomi talked about during their drive to Oakland Due Avenue. Judas was waiting for them at the entrance of their apartment when Sydney and Naomi arrived, he stood taller than Sydney had imagined and she was utterly taken back by the sex appeal Judas oozed. "I'm just walking into trouble ain't I?" Sydney uttered under her breath, and catching his eye through the window. "What's that Syd?" Naomi asked before she cut off her engine and unbuckled her seat belt. She was grinning ear to ear. "Nothing, I umm, it just feels good to be home." Sydney lied as Naomi got out the car. She watched as Judas greeted Naomi by kissing her cheek, and then turned to help her retrieve the luggage Sydney had piled up in her sisters trunk. Naomi wasn't lying when she said Judas was Fine. "Yeah, were definitely jumping on his sexy ass!" Sydney said, and then as if she'd burped covered her mouth. That had been happening a lot lately. Her personalities had found a way to manipulate her speech and every so often they spoke their minds. "Damn. You weren't lying Nay. It's like looking at your twin!" Judas had said to Naomi when she'd formally introduced him to Sydney. Sydney wanted to burst out laughing because it was obvious that Judas was checking her out. She silently thanked God as she followed behind both Judas and Naomi, for guiding her in the right direction when she'd chosen the outfit she'd worn that afternoon. Her tight fitting, leopard-skin, print jumpsuit was one of a few sexy outfits she owned, and this was the first time it had been shown a good time. "Right, you're all set." Judas said, and placed the last of Sydney's suitcases in her new room. He heading down the hall, and then stopped in mid thought. "Nay I'm gonna take a quick shower." He turned around and said. "Nice to meet you Sydney and it's good to have you home." He politely added before leaving the women alone. Sydney watched Judas's broad shoulders and tight ass disappear into what she presumed to be him and Naomi's bedroom, and wondered what it would be like to have her legs wrapped around his waist. "I told you he was gorgeous didn't I." Naomi joked. She slapped Sydney playfully seeing her checking out her man, and they shared a light laugh before Naomi made for the door. "Listen" She interjected the mood. "I gotta make a quick run to Queens. I got a double-booked customer I need to tend to then, I'll come back and we can grab something to eat. If you need anything, my numbers on the phone, or you can speak to Judas he's gonna be here all day, and he don't bite." Naomi said on her way to the door, and then she was gone. Sydney left her bedroom and wandered through the apartment starting with the kitchen that opened out into the lounge. She flicked through the CDs on the rack next to one of the large black, floor speakers, and nodded her head in approval at the wide music collection her sister and Judas kept, until the sound of water pressure from the shower filled the apartment. And something inside her stirred. Sydney had Paige to thank for her interception between Judas and herself. Their relationship since then had been nothing but relentless joy and content. Judas made love to Sydney's mind. With him, Sydney learnt to tame and keep a hold of the minds she owned. They were content with her choice, unlike they had been with her Ex, and Judas satisfied them all up to an extent.

When Sydney changed around Judas, she always seemed to change to meet his frame of mind. It was like the personalities within her surrendered themselves to both his mental and physical needs, and in return Judas was so in love with Sydney that he was begging for her to have his seed. "Judas must think I'm a fool if he's thinks he's gonna have me bare-footed, and pregnant like the rest of his babymother's." Sydney said to herself on her way to the fridge. She pulled a carton of orange juice off the shelf and placed it on the counter, so she could retrieve her medication, and take her first dosage for the day. "What the... Where the hell is my shit?" She muttered when she didn't see the three oval containers her medication was keep in inside the cupboard above the stove. 'This has got to be a joke.' She threw her hands up in the air, and stomped back to the bathroom where Naomi had moved her medication to before. "Why would I put my pills in the bathroom?" Sydney spoke out aloud to herself, cursing Naomi for moving her pills. "Who's gonna pop a pill while they're brushing their teeth, or taking a shit?" She said standing on the toilet seat and becoming level with the cupboard above the sink. She stood there for what seemed like an eternity, with her hand on the wall, staring at what she'd found. Tears instantly began running down her face, and a surge of energy passed through her body causing her to lose her footing and fall. "HOW COULD YOU?" Sydney shouted, busting into Naomi's office, and pounded her desk while waving a pregnancy test in the air. "My God Sydney, give me that. Naomi leapt around her desk, and grabbed her sister whispering in her sister's ear. "Where is your medication?"

She could hear the ruckus her customers were making downstairs, they were rightfully alarmed, and wondering what the hell was going on. Sydney had jumped into a cab, and stormed full speed ahead through Queens, and into Naomi's office wearing a bath towel and dripping wet. Naomi pried the stick out of Sydney's hand and asked Judas to look around for something for Sydney to wear, and when he left the room Sydney fell silent, and tranquil. She knew she was partly to blame for Judas deception. She had to take responsibility for trusting him. But it was hard. Especially seeing as she had been so convinced that Judas's commitment and dedication to their relationship was real. Sydney used the back of her hands, and wiped her eyes clear of the tears that fogged her vision, and stood half naked in the middle of the room. Her whole world was falling apart, and the fucked up thing about it was that it had just begun to get better. Sydney had given Judas herself and more, and he had committed an ultimate betrayal. Sure it was no secret that he had children crawling all over London, but this was a blow to the heart. Not only had Judas lied, but he'd left Sydney no choice but to end the relationship they'd begun to build. There was no way she could live in the same house as her lover's love child, not to mention a child which she shared the same blood. 'If he's lied to us about this, what else is he keeping from us?' 'You done fucked it up for the rest of us now, bitch.' 'I told you not to trust 'em.' Sydney heard the voices in her head taunt before she could keep their thoughts from slipping from her own tongue. Out of nowhere carnage and mayhem had broken out in Naomi's office, and for a short moment, if only a second Naomi managed to find peace knowing that she was with child. Eight years she'd tried to conceive and failed, whilst hood rats and junkies pushed their buggies freely about the hood. Sydney had fallen pregnant in the past, but that was something they never talked about, even now, so it was inconsiderate for Naomi to leave something so sensitive lying around the house, especially with Sydney's condition and her not bothering to take her meds. Still it was no excuse for Sydney to behave the way she did in public, least of all in Naomi's place of work. Naomi surfaced up a smile and sent it Essen's way. She was glad when he'd gotten up from his seat to answer to the door as the knocking had begun to get on her last nerve. She'd warned her sister of the repercussions she'd have if she'd neglected to take her proscribed medication, but as usual, Sydney had failed to listen, and now here she was struggling with her mental disorder all over again. She looked exhausted, thirsty and pale, and evidently cared nothing for the dark bags she sported under her eyes. Naomi remembered what it was like constantly having to tend to the needs of a medicated schizophrenic, that's why she'd purposely neglected to mention the symptoms Sydney experienced as a result of her mental disorder to Judas upon bring Sydney home. If he'd known about her hallucinations, bizarre delusions, and disorganized speech and neglected to her moving in, then the dissociative identity disorder she persistently hid would have defiantly revised his decision for her to stay. "You stupid whore!" Sydney shouted. Unaware that the voices in her head had yet again, manipulated her speech. "You stupid, stupid whore!" She repeated over and over again whilst sobbing out loud. Naomi put her arm around her sister's neck, she held Sydney in her arms as she trembled, and used her free hand to smooth her hair into place. Judas crept back into the office, and held out a shirt that he'd found, and Naomi motioned for him to sit down. The last thing she wanted him to do was leave. She didn't have the energy to deal with Sydney on her own, and began, holding back tears of her own. Naomi blamed herself for releasing Sydney back into the custody of the Cleverfield Mental Home at eighteen, while she was struggling with her diagnosis of DID. The professional's had convinced Naomi that DID was curable, and that Sydney would be home before the summer came to an end. But that never happened. Sydney was heavily medicated after numerous attempts to escape, and only now, at twenty- five, was she deemed stable enough to settle back into what they called 'normal life'. "It's okay Syd, your home now." Naomi said rocking her sister in her arms. She then looked over at Judas who had yet to speak through Sydney's emotional ordeal. Naomi put it down to him not wanting to get involved in what he called "Women's business", which was ironic, because he hadn't thought like that before he'd messed with Naomi's account.

Chapter 15

Samantha had knocked on Naomi's office door a dozen times in the last hour, but nobody answered, nor did they rush to the door. Their ruckus, though muffled could be heard from the bottom of the stairs and, had begun to cause chatter amongst the clients and staff. So, she knocked again, this time with her whole fist, and she kept pounding on the door until a shadow appeared in the frosted window, and the handle turned. Essen's scent came out the office, and wrapped itself around her before he did. "Thank God Essen. What the hell's going on in there? I need to speak to Naomi now! Shit's getting crazy out here!" Samantha stood on her toes and explained. She tried her best to nosey past Essen, to get a glimpse of what all the shouting was about, but Essen stood at 6ft 2", and blocked the entire doorway, allowing only the sounds of disagreement and confrontation to pass. "For real Sam, you don't even wanna talk to Naomi right now. If you think shit's crazy out here then you don't want none of what's popping off in there" Essen joked. Closing the door behind him, and put his arm around Samantha's shoulder. Together they descended back down the stairs. "How you been girl, keeping outta trouble I hope?" He said, making convosation. Samantha and Essen, like Judas all attended the same secondary school, Hackney Grove Community High (CGCH). So it was nothing for two old friends to brief each other on the circumstances they'd been presented with in life. "You mean besides running Naomi's business single handily, and bring up two teenage thugs on my own. Same old shit, just a different day right?" Samantha recited Rick Ross's 'Blowing Money' joint, and playfully replied as they reached the bottom of the stairs. "Yeah beside's all that?" Essen laughed. "How's Spider, I know you and the boys are looking forward to him coming home." He referred to her incarcerated husband, and his good-friend. Quincy 'Spider' Clarke was an old skool member of their team. In fact, he was one of the first. Spider ran with Judas and his boy's before selling crack came to mind. Before the law got devious and crooked, Spider's reputation was large. He was Judas's original collector. No debt was absentmindedly left unpaid when Spider ran the streets. He collected with a firm hand, but never abused his position. So it was fucked up when Spider was arrested, and taken away from the premises of his home. The police had beat him senseless in the street before they established he was without a weapon, and then to add insult to injury, they had him shipped out of the district which cut his visits from his wife and kids. "I know you and your brothers looking forward to your dad coming home. Right little man?" Essen stopped and said to Samantha's son on his way to the door. Kieran looked up from his phone and made eye contact with his mother's male friend. He hardly acknowledged the man's comment before he sized him up and looked away. "Rah..." Essen checked himself and chuckled. "Your gonna have to watch that one," Essen laughed at the tuff expression posted on the young boys face. He and Samantha finished off their conversation whilst making their way to the front of the salon. They stopped briefly at the door before he unlocked his car and got in, still talking, but adamant to make a move. "You take care of yourself out there, and don't be a stranger, pop your head in sometimes." Samantha shouted out to him before he shut his car door and secured himself with his belt. He watched the hustle and bustle of the salon's workers and clientele in silence through the closed window of his car. Samantha had long returned to her station whilst Mariah stood centre attention of a small group of females leaving the rest of the employees of Queens switching from client to client to manage their heavy load of work. Essen took one last glance at Queen's before putting his car in drive, he watched the same Chinese woman who hustled in the car park in Tesco's pull a wad of DVD's out her coat and attempt to sell them amongst the clients and staff in the Salon, then thought about what Judas had said to Naomi. How they'd talk about what it was she'd wrote down on that piece of paper at home. He knew what it meant for Naomi when Judas spoke with that tone. But Essen being Judas's boy would never question Judas regarding what he considered being 'his boy's biz'. He was on his way to meet Sensi, this time not to take orders, but to give a piece of his mind. He knew that whatever it was Judas had done, Sensi would bring from the darkness into the light. It had become a profitable profession of his to assist the Mendez's when they found themselves backed up against a wall.

Chapter 16

"Where did I go wrong?' Naomi silently asked herself whilst she sat on the edge on her desk, with her legs dangling over the edge. She rubbed her sister gently on the back as she sniffled besides her. 'Why does my family's needs always have to come before mine? I've been here before, taking care of Sydney, spoon feeding her medication. I can't do it no more. She's a grown-ass woman for god's sake.' She wanted to scream. It had taken her years to get rid of the stench her family had left on her name. Her father had been killed and labeled a murderer, her mother smoked crack, Johnson, her older brother was serving time in prison, and her baby sister Sydney was a medicated psycho set out to destroy everything she'd worked for. Naomi and Judas were happy before Sydney had moved in. In fact, they were the happiest they'd been in years. They'd traveled to the South of France just a week before Sydney had arrived, and when they'd gotten back Judas has spoiled Naomi with a surprise. He knew she'd had her eyes on a pearl BMW X5, but the man on the floor of the showroom in West Ham said that the X5 only came in white. It was like having the old

Judas back, after all the fighting they'd been doing created by the lifestyle they lived in the streets. It took a lot out of Naomi to get Judas to be content. When a new car hit the floor Judas would be the man on the streets owning the ride, his shit always had to be bigger and better than everybody else's, and the more people that talked about him, the more bossy he got. That made Naomi careful of his team. Her father was a man with Judas's wealth, and it was a debate within his team that Naomi believed eventually saw him killed. Naomi's father was a humble man, but loved his family with wealth. Sydney coughed and caught Naomi's attention. She looked at her watch and then turned to the knocking at her door. If there was anything Naomi hated more, it was going to the hairdressers when the sun was rising and leaving when it had begun to set. Women would go as far as booking a 6:45am appointment just so they could get their shit straight before they bumped into the slick looking delivery boy on their way to their office or desks. Every woman knew when putting an outfit together the hair was what made the pretty picture. Be it long, short, or curly, if your hair was jacked up, then so will be your day. It had taken Naomi the best part of her Saturday to get her finances in order and her sister in check, Samantha had covered her appointments for the morning and now she was needed at a station as Mariah had disappeared like she usually did during her shift. "Hold on Samantha," Naomi said once she'd opened the door. Samantha stood in at the top of the stairs her brows in a frown and frustration lines on her forehead. She nodded and turned, descending back down the stairs. Naomi had undoubtedly pushed her employees and Samantha was due a break, so with Sydney now calm her eyes pleaded with Judas to keep her stable whilst she attended to the ruckus in the Salon. But this time Naomi made her escape with Sydney's best interested in mind, she fears if she had to stay stifled in that room with her past any longer, she wouldn't be able to stop herself from speaking her mind. "I got this." Judas mouthed, feeling a little uneasy with the situation at hand. He was sure that when Sydney had come in soaking wet and shouting insults he was busted, but in her voice something wasn't right. It wasn't like Sydney to curse herself out, especially in such an extraordinary manner. Judas had had women turn crazy over him plenty times before, but this was different. Judas looked over at Sydney exhausted, and curled up in the long leather chair at the far end of the room and sighed. He was never good with raw emotions, Sydney's outburst had thrown him off guard, but he loved her. More than even he knew until then. He reluctantly rose from his chair and strode slowly towards Sydney with his hands buried in his pockets and his head hung in shame. There was something very different about the way she looked that afternoon. While her physical appearance remained the same, her hair, eyes and facial expressions differed from the Sydney he knew. "I don't know what to say Syd, I'm sorry!" Judas stood before her apologizing from the heart. The tension in the room was killing him. It had been almost 8 years since he had stood before a woman he loved, having to tell her another woman was carrying his child. "Why you crying baby? We can work this out...Right?" He asked becoming agitated with her silence. Sydney shifted in her chair, and sat up; she used the back of her hands to wipe her tear stricken face. Judas was talking to her, she was sure of it. His mouth moved as did he, yet the only words Sydney heard were those that were in her head. "He betrayed us Syd and now you're gonna sit back and let him betray Naomi too?" "If you walk now, Naomi needs never know that you fucked her man!" "She's gonna find out some day, I say follow this shit through keep fucking the nigga so we can stack this money. I got a plan girl!" "How could you do this to us?" Sydney snapped back into reality and said. While whimpering; she was fully aware that she was falling back into her old ways. Slipping from personality to personality within the time it took for a person to blink their eyes. The medication she was prescribed to take daily by the Cleverfield Mental Home made her drowsy and numb, the first dosage of Chlorpromazine she took in the morning knocked her out cold for at least three hours of the day, whilst the Escitalopram and Lithium Carbonate left her an empty shell. She didn't feel like anybody, not Sydney, or the other three personalities that emerged on occasion, contributing to the decisions she made every day. Judas sat down on the soft, Italian leather chair, next to Sydney and watched curiously as she calmly placed a hair band she had around her wrist into her hair, pulling it back into a wet, frizzy, ponytail. "I'm sorry!" Judas whispered. "I never meant for this to happen, and I sure as hell didn't ask for this baby." It hurt him to see Sydney so distraught over him. The last thing he wanted to do was break her heart. He irritably got up and walked to the window with his back hunched. "This is the last thing I fucking need." He stood there and thought, listening to Sydney's sniffles, and looking down onto the street below. He watched Essen pull off, and race down Upper Street, and wondered where he was heading. He and Essen had remained tight since secondary school, yet unlike him Essen never had a separating business from pleasure. "When did you start sleeping with her?" Sydney asked. She snuck up behind Judas and startled him with her question. Her anguish had turned into rage. "You know what, don't answer that. You got me fucked up enough with your lies." "Shelly was right your playing us both, and there I was feeling guilty. Thinking that you were the better partner in you and Naomi's relationship, that you were neglected and hurt, but I guess that was just more game huh?" "Syd, I'm..." Judas tried to cut in, but Sydney was having none of it. "You're what? Save it Judas, you fucking me and my sister." Sydney said mad. "Man, I can't believe I trusted you!" She used all her strength to push Judas as hard as she could. He stumbled, slightly, but regained his balance and grabbed Sydney before she could lash out at him again. "Lower you fucking voice." He whispered in her ear whilst restraining her in a bear like hold. "Who said you couldn't trust me, this don't change shit. All it means is that we need to start making some moves." "Moves?" Sydney struggled in his arms confused. Judas blinked and she was gone. "Syd I'm dead serious. I admit that I lied about sleeping with Naomi that was a mistake, but I wasn't lying when I told you how I felt about you, and that my relationship with her was dead." "Us!" Sydney corrected. "How you felt about us!" "Yeah us," Judas stopped pacing to look at her. She still looked different, but then she had been crying, so he went on. "We gotta do this right." "Naomi being pregnant might work to our advantage. She can't be less than four or five months." He thought out aloud. He neglected to mention the passionate night he'd spent with Naomi when Sydney had gone out. There was no point throwing salt in Sydney's wounds not now that she was quiet, and he had her attention. Besides, the lack thereof he and Naomi's sex-life couldn't place her pregnancy any later than that. "In a couple more months, Naomi's gonna be run of her feet, nausea, Braxton hicks all that shits gonna kick in, leaving us to do our thing. I got it all planned out Syd, I been sitting on this thought for a hot minute, and it feels right. I just gotta pull some last strings, and we're good." "You just promise me your down for the long haul and I got you." Judas looked into Sydney eyes and said. "I don't understand Judas." Sydney felt her voice rise and heard herself say. "Are we talking about business or us?" "Both." Judas said, "If I've gotta walk away from Naomi to be with you then I'm not leaving empty handed." He tried to worked game, but Sydney wasn't alone seeing past his comfort words. "I've managed to have Naomi's name removed from everything except Queens, but I will. Right now I'm in the process of seeking legal advice for obtaining sole rights to the Block. I've started investing Syd, and I'm investing big." He told her excitedly. And Sydney listened "I met this old school dude down in a bar about a year ago, he works in construction, building and shit, and he owns a major shipping deport in London. We got talking for some time, and he kinda reminded me of an O.G. except he didn't have any baggage or educational stories. He was straight up cool, so we exchanged numbers then went our separate ways." "I mean, it was a little while after you came to stay that he contacted me and asked if I was still interested in expanding my work. I told him that I was into street pharmaceuticals." Judas chuckled. He had their future all planned out. Using his new partners company he could deliver his product anywhere in the country without suspicion and aggravation from the law. He still planned on keeping his lab running in the block and working alongside his father to rob and cut down the main distributors in their town. Without those attributes, he had no product. "He's gonna put me straight, no more taking orders or playing by the rules." Judas continued. Someone in Sydney liked the idea of that. Her heart fluttered, and although she didn't want to something willed her to love him. All this time she'd thought that he hadn't even played with the thought of leaving Naomi and making it happen with her, but she was wrong, Shelly was wrong and so was Brittany. Sure it was gonna be uncomfortable living in the apartment knowing that she and Judas were planning on ducking out, but it would only be a matter of time before Naomi dropped her load. Sydney took a moment to gather her thoughts; she remembered what Shelly had said. 'This ain't the type of situation that ends in tears Syd.' "I know, but I'm already in too deep." She mumbled to herself. It was crazy going over the pros and cons of the situation, Sydney knew no matter what she told herself she'd just find an excuse to over ride her pride. She looked up at him, staring point blank into his eyes. She wished they could tell her what she was getting herself into, but they were cold. The only information she had that told her what she was dealing with was the crumpled post-it note Judas had allowed to slip out of his hand when he'd sat next to her in the leather chair. Sydney held it tight in her hand. She'd snuck a peek at the figure scribbled down in Naomi's hand writing and knew then that she'd scored big. She couldn't care less about taking Naomi out of the game and stealing her position on the board. She should have held down her position, but instead she was taken out by a pawn. 'He should have kept it real with us Syd, don't trust him!' 'I'll tell you what were gonna do!' Sydney shook her head to rid herself of the debate in her mind. "How do I know you ain't gonna shit on me like you're doing to Naomi?" She enquired and awaited Judas's reply. Sydney was still deeply in love with Judas, and though the personalities within her thought he was a snake she was determined to prove them wrong. "Come on Syd, what we got is real." Judas shifted nervously on his feet. "In a couple of months I'll be asking you the same thing." Sydney and her others were all ears. "You're the only person I trust Syd," Judas grabbed Sydney's face and kissed her genially on the lips. "That's why I'm putting everything in your name.

Sydney's heart almost dropped out of her ass, she desperately tried to pull away from him, but a stronger force within her wouldn't let go. Judas had stirred, inside Sydney a mental war. Her mouth curled up into a smile and she looked him dead in the eyes, trying to contain a deceitful laugh. Naomi should have warned him that her sister was the queen of playing, dirty, mind games, and his small figurine was no match for her player on the board.

Chapter 17

"You're father and I should have thrown you out a long time ago, you thieving little bitch!" Mrs. Swindle shouted down from her bedroom window as Shelly pulled up to the pavement outside Brittany's house, and stopped at a halt. Shelly presumed that Brittany had been up to her old tricks, dipping into her parents savings jar despite their attempts to hide it, and she was right. Mrs. Swindle had exposed that she had taken almost fourteen hundred pounds in the last month alone, and had no way, or intentions to pay it back. For Brittany, it wasn't easy being a high maintenance white chick that lived in the hood, but so far she'd managed like her mother, and her mother before her- to get away with never working a day in her life. "Don't you dare think about bringing your ass back here without a job, or me and your father's money!" Shelly heard Brittany's mother say before Brittany ran out the house and down the stoop, slamming the front door behind her. "Just get me the hell out of here." Brittany said after throwing herself in the passenger's seat of Shelly's Nisan Micra. She closed her eyes and allowed thought's of her relationship with Craig to cloud her mind. She couldn't think of anything that would cause him to disappear, or why he hadn't called her to let her know where he was at. Where the hell is that fool? She thought to herself, frustrated and angry, all at the same time. She and Craig had been going steady for the past year until the previous weekend. No one had so much as heard from him over the previous week, and Brittany was beginning to panic with concern. It was no use calling him day or night as her calls went straight to the voice mail. A single tear rolled over Brittany's cheek, and she used the back of her hand to quickly wipe it away. Brittany Swindle never allowed a man to get under her skin, but she had to admit that Craig had her sprung. She held him down through his four-month bid behind the wall, and even had one of her girls who worked in a bank hook his sister up with a job when his family fell on hard times. That was how she obtained her cheque books, but with Craig, it wasn't even about the money. They had a nice little stash together, and Brittany didn't mind a little hustle, she quite preferred making money on her own terms. "Cheer up Britt." Shelly said after a long, uncomfortable, silence. "It might never happen." "What?" Brittany turned to her friend and mumbled, she hadn't noticed that Shelly was talking to her she was so lost in thought. "I said cheer up. After we get Sydney from Queens we'll work on getting your parents money back. We got enough time to hit Westfield right?" Shelly asked concentrating on the road. "I don't give a fuck about my parent's money and neither do they." Brittany said. She sank deeper in her chair and sighed. "I'm done." "Done, what'd you mean done?" Shelly asked, she took her eyes off the road a few seconds, and placed her palm on Brittany's forehead to see if she was sick "Don't tell me your gonna let a nigga like Craig throw you off your game?" She said with sarcasm. Brittany was the last person in the world Shelly expected to get emotional over a man, especially a guy like Craig. His long, lanky, structure wasn't Brittany's usual type, and the brother stayed ashy through all four seasons of the year, it was a myth why Brittany was tripping so hard over his ass. But tears flowed freely down Brittany's cheeks, and by the time Shelly had parked up Brittany's make-up was a mess. "I fucked up this time Shelly." Brittany admitted, her chest heaving up, and down as she struggled to control her breathing. She pulled a spliff out of a cigarette box she had in her purse and lit it with trembling hands. "You know I fuck with nigga's right?" She flicked ash out the window then turned back to Shelly and asked. "Yeah course," Shelly nodded everybody who knew Brittany, knew she milked brothers like cows, yet they were still her biggest fans. She fucked with drug dealers, fraudsters, robbers and hustlers by trade, none of these men were considered exclusive, educated self-respecting black men, so Shelly called them nigga's, the government's definition to the next black generation. "So you know what's up then. Like, I mean you know how I get mines right?" Brittany asked curious to see how much her best friend knew about her promiscuous ways. "Come on Britt, I know what you're about," Shelly said, declining Brittany's offer of a pull from her joint. It was way too early in the day for Shelly to get high. "What's all that got to do with you fucking up though?" She asked. "I fucked things up for the both of us Shell! I fucking loved that boy, and instead of handling my business and keeping it moving I slipped up." Her voice cracked, "I fell in love with him and he fucked me over. He fucked us both over." She cried. Shelly now understood Brittany's pain, but she knew hers would be greater. If she didn't have this week's money then, her ass was Bradley's, and Angela didn't play games. Shelly didn't know what to say. "Are you sure Syd told you to get me before you picked her up?" Brittany changed the subject. She noticed they were parked opposite Queens, and today was one of those days when she unburdened her heart. "Listen we can't talk about this here, but Sydney's got us a little earners for next weekend. Okay so it's nothing glamorous like your runs, just collecting shit and dropping it off, but Syd said she'll handle the dropping off part while me and you hold her down by tagging along." "You know, you two need to put all this competitive shit behind you and focus on what's happening now, Syd knows moneys tight, I couldn't help but tell her about Bradley and Angela's threats but listen, were picking her up now, and she'll explain the program to you like she did me, and you'll be pleased to know that what Sydney's got up her sleeve may not be my cup of tea, but it sounded right up your street, Judas is playing king, and I know you been waiting or your opportunity to fuck with a couple of members in his crew." Shelly said hoping to change Brittany's miserable mood. But it didn't. "You know me Shell, I'm down for whatever's putting money in my purse, but you know Syd and I ain't exactly vybzing right. Our friendship just ain't the same anymore. She doesn't talk to me the way she used to, and you two seem so close that sometimes I feel like I am just tagging along. You know, for old time sake." Again Shelly didn't know what to say, there was nothing she could say to restrain the way Brittany felt. Shelly and Sydney had kept in constant contact while Sydney was at the Cleverfield Mental Home and had become closer than they ever was, Brittany wasn't there when Sydney needed her most, she was out chasing hood dreams , so their friendship had its flaws. "Here wipe your face." Shelly said throwing Brittany a baby-wipe she'd taken out of the glove compartment. She had parked across the street from Queens, just in time to see Judas leaving Queens. Earlier that afternoon Sydney had called Shelly and confided in her over the phone about Naomi's pregnancy, and the plan Judas had to expand his empire with her by his side. Usually Shelly wouldn't have condoned such an unorthodox plan, but Kaylen had a plan of his own. During Sydney's stay at the Cleverfield Mental Home, whilst she was being monitored without sedatives, Sydney made an unbreakable pact. She'd reasoned with her thriving personalities, and begged them to give her peace. The doctors and nurses must have thought she was straight crazy, cursing, and shouting demands. But Sydney had known for years that they were a part of her, and would be, until the day she died. Two of the three agreed to play by the rules, while one of them wanted to graft. An over protective, fierce personality who'd kill for the ones he loved. He'd never forgotten his father's fall, and was determined to restore his family's good name. Judas was a mere stepping stone into the game, because there was a new player on the board Kaylen Henderson AKA Kane. "Aye Judas, what's up?" Brittany shouted out the passenger window. She waved her hand signaling for him to come over before he had a chance to get into his car. "Great..." Shelly mumbled, and sunk down in her seat rolling her eyes. While she planned to profit from Sydney's ambitious plan, she hated Judas, and had made it clear that under no circumstances ought she to be acquainted with him and his team. She was there for Sydney, and her own financial needs. She wasn't trying to get caught up in whatever games Judas seemed to be playing "What's up girls, Brittany, right?" Judas asked after he'd crossed street. Brittany was blatantly, checking Judas out, she sized him up real good before licking her lips and flirting. "Yeah I'm Brittany, but can call me Britt. Everyone else does. It's nice to finally meet you in person though Judas, we've heard so much about you." "Ain't we Shell?" She blew smoke and nudged Shelly in the arm. Shelly looked up at Judas and flashed him a fake smile. "Is that right Brittany?" Judas took the spliff out of Brittany's hand and flirted before placing it to his own lips. He ignored the lack of enthusiasm from her friend and leaned into Brittany's open window, blowing smoke into the car. His fragrance had her wide open and she felt herself drifting towards him for the full pleasure of his scent. She knew Judas was Naomi's man but damn he was fine. She couldn't even front, if she hadn't caught Sydney fucking Judas the other night, had she had the chance, she would have been riding his dick too. "Yeah, but I mean, a girl can never know too much!" Brittany flirted right back. "Sydney said..." "Here she comes right now..." Shelly abruptly cleared her throat, before

Sydney threw herself into the back seat, and Brittany had a chance to bate her up. "Are we just gonna sit here?" Sydney asked cutting Judas a nasty look, and urging Shelly to pull off. "I'll catch up with you girls later." Judas stood and said. He slowly turned and headed for his own car. "What the hell happened to you, and why you half dressed in the middle of the day?" Brittany threw Sydney a pack of baby-wipes that landed hard in Sydney's chest, and raised her brow. "You know what, I ain't trying to have you two cat-fighting in my car." Shelly warned after Sydney had hit Brittany back. "Oh please..." Brittany screeched. "A few cat scratched would be a face lift on this piece of shit." Sydney snickered, and so did Shelly deep down. She pulled out of her spot and headed East with Judas trailing behind. "So what's this money play you got?" Brittany changed the subject. Sydney's eyes lit up at the mention of money and she wasted no time bring Brittany up to speed. Judas had another thing coming if he thought he was gonna play Sydney like he had done her sister, neither of them had been more to him than a holding account with a pretty face. "It's as simple as this..."Sydney began. She pulled her loose hair back in one. Shelly had even stopped the car. She'd never seen Sydney so tense. Both Shelly and Brittany were all ears. "Were about to teach Mr. Mendez a lesson in respect, and while we're at it I'm gonna teach him a little sum 'thing about deceit.

Chapter 18

Sydney, Shelly and Brittany entered the elevator of Judas and Naomi's apartment building in Oakland Due Avenue, laughing and joking about the good old days. Some of the best times they'd had were when they were young, carefree, and single teens. "How's my Niece doing?" Sydney asked Shelly half annoyed. Brittany had waited just long enough for the elevator doors to close before she filled the confined space with thick, intoxicating, smoke. "Oh now you wanna know how your niece is?" Shelly joked. "I swear sometimes it's like she was mothered and fathered by the both of you." She pointed to both Sydney and Brittany who both fell out laughing because they knew they were stuck in their ways, and Shelly's daughter Special was just as bad. "I hear she's got a little attitude now." Sydney said. "Syd, Special was born with an attitude." Shelly laughed as the elevator came to a halt, and opened onto the 19th floor. Brittany had created a fog in the elevator, but it was nothing compared to the harsh clouds of air that struck their lungs when they walked into the apartment, and towards the kitchen where everyone had congregated. Judas waved them over, and everyone in the room at one time, or another, stopped what they were doing long enough to acknowledge their presence by raising their heads. Sydney took a seat next to Judas followed by Brittany while Shelly nervously settled into her seat. "Hey, I'm Jada." A slender, gum popping, Spanish woman stuck her hand out for them all to shake. "What's up?" She said with each shake. "But umm, everybody calls me Cook." She winked, and went about introducing Judas's team. "That's Julius right there." Cook pointed to a chubby teenage boy who oddly resembled Judas. "And them right there is Nugget, Leo, Spades, and Trina." "You girls already know Essen right?" Jada clicked her tongue as she spoke. "And of course Judas doesn't need an introduction." She rubbed his shoulders seductively, and giggled, much to Sydney's dislike. Judas saw her face drop and immediately shook Jada off. "What! You forgot about your boy already Cookie?" A sizeable figure said, making his way through the smoke. Everybody turned in their seats to the man approaching the table. As he got closer the smoke cleared, and into plan view came Sticks. "You're the man, Bruv I appreciate you looking out." Sticks dapped Essen as he walked past him into the smoke filled apartment. "Don't even mention it," Essen coldly answered, and half-heartedly held his fist out. Nugget and Spades pounded Sticks whilst he settled himself around the table. They wasted no time bringing him up to speed with the latest street saga while he lustfully made eyes at Brittany. Brittany helped herself to the free flowing weed, and alcohol while intensively listening to the chatter within the room. "I thought you said we were having a meeting." Shelly whispered to Sydney. "Yes girls we are!" Judas answered turning his attention away from his conversation with Essen. He turned around in his chair and took the last drag of his spliff before putting it out. "Syd, you sure you want to do this?" Judas asked Sydney. She looked at her girls then back at Judas, and nodded 'Yes'. "Then I'm gonna pull you three in." He winked "So long as you keep what you hear in this house where it's heard." He warned. Sydney, Shelly and Brittany nodded their heads in unison and waited for Judas to go on, and he got straight to the point. "Occasionally 'Nice' people can be perceived as naïve or tolerant. I can assure you that that isn't the case with us. We're all nice people ain't that right guys?" He said to his fellow crew. They all agreed with him, egging him on. He stopped and poured himself a drink. "We're trustworthy, and we give generously, with the understanding that all debts must be paid, but, things don't always work out like that." Judas stood and said. He took a swig of his drink before placing his glass back on the table, then paced the floor as he spoke. "We've all been there, right? Missed a rent payment, fell back on the electric bill." Shelly nodded her head in agreement whilst Brittany rolled her eyes. "Well this game ain't the electric company or the fucking council, it's bigger than that. I'd say it's more like..." He paused for thought. "Life insurance," Sticks said completing Judas's sentence. "Yeah, life insurance, I never thought of it like that." Judas continued. "But that's exactly what it is, except this is the type of insurance that insures your life." He guzzled his drink down, and the cleared his throat. "When a member of the public comes to me for financial help it's my duty to put them on, but if for some reason, or the other they fall behind on their payments, or they simply disappear then I simply have no choice but to send in my own personal team of collectors to retrieve the remaining balance of the debt, and I can't always be held accountable for the manner of which it's retrieved." All eyes in the room were on him. "Look, no offence or anything. But, what's all that got to do with us?" Brittany asked. She rose from her chair with her arms folded. Most of the cats from the hood she messed with were drug dealers or made mad money knocking people off, so she'd been around enough criminal activities to follow Judas's line of work. "Sit down!" Sydney gritted through her teeth. "Nah, she can stand. She has every right to do as she pleases." Judas said. Sticks stood from his chair and stood directly behind the chair that once accommodated Brittany's ass. "Yeah she can stand." Sticks repeated aroused. He sent chills up Brittany's spine. Essen felt sick watching Sticks. He inhaled Brittany's fragrance while her eyes followed him as he circled her, watching her every move. "You scared?" Sticks caught her watching and whispered in her ear. Brittany nodded 'No' right before Essen cleared his throat. Judas poured himself another drink. "Where was I?" He asked. "You said something about Collectors." Julius answered. He couldn't be more than fifteen, yet he sat listening intensively to the words that were coming out of the men's mouths. "That's right younger, my personal team of collectors. Imagine how I felt when my man called me and told me that I no longer had to trace missing policy holders who'd fled without paying their debt.

Him doing all the Detective work for me spares a lot of free time for the team. Besides..." Judas looked at Sydney while he spoke "Collection is easy. And since you girls are related to my girl you're fam, it wouldn't be right for me not to put you on." "What happen to your last collectors?" Shelly reluctantly asked. Her voice cracked when she spoke but, she had to ask, she wasn't risking putting herself in any kind of uncompromising position that screamed danger. Special needed her mother more than they needed the money.' It needs to be worth the risk,' Shelly thought, as did Brittany and she the same. "I ain't gonna lie girls, this ain't the kind of work that comes without risk. But I can assure you that your safety will be my first and foremost priority when sending you into the wild." "The wild!" Brittany streaked with sarcasm. "Boy, please... I know these streets like the back of my hand, and there ain't nothing wild out there we ain't ever seen." "Well go ahead and handle your business." Judas said applauding Brittany's cold heart. He liked a woman who had a bit of fight in their bones, and was confident when it came to putting in work. Sydney and her girls were perfect for the job. They seemed obedient and loyal, still Judas made a mental note to keep a watchful eye on Brittany and her self-assured attitude as he saw a liability waiting to explode. He removed himself from around the kitchen table, and disappeared into the master room. His team all picked up with the conversations they were having amongst themselves until Judas, in almost no time at all, returned to the kitchen with paper items in his hands. "This right here is gonna get you in the establishment where your target has been scheduled to be." He said when he returned, holding three tickets to Elite - The biggest gambling venue in the West End. "Now! You want us to take care of this now?" Sydney asked confused. The tickets that Judas placed in front of Sydney, accompanied by written instructions were dated for that night. "It ain't like there's nothing out there you ain't ever seen." Sticks repeated what Brittany had said earlier. Brittany cut her eyes at him, and followed behind Sydney as she and Shelly made their way to her room. "What an asshole." Brittany whispered to Shelly then turned to look back at Sticks, who despite hearing what she'd said smiled, and raised his glass her way. *** "These people are dangerous Syd," Shelly said when herself, Sydney and Brittany were in the privacy of Sydney's room. "Not once did you mention anything about murder." she paced the room, replaying in her mind what Judas had said. "This is the type of insurance that insures your life." "I ain't feeling this either," Brittany sucked her teeth and sat down on the edge of the bed. "Calm down, shit! Nobody said anything about murder, all we gotta do is find this Smiley, retrieve his stash, and hand it back to Judas at the end of the night." Sydney tried to explain, whilst reading the instructions Judas had given her in the other room. "You did hear what happened to the last collector's right?" Shelly asked. "No Shelly and neither did you." Sydney replied. She knew Shelly was nervous, hell, she was nervous too. "I don't like the sound of this Syd. You know men don't like people fucking with their money." Shelly said. But Kaylen was ready to put in work. He cared nothing for the love that Sydney felt for the man he'd deemed had fooled them all. Sitting back and watching his outer persona attract a vulture sickened him. He'd watched his father through Sydney's eyes build an upstanding, family-orientated empire, alongside a flock of hard-working members of the community that ordained respect. It was devastating for Kaylen to see everything his father worked for destroyed, and his family name tarnished along with it. Like his father, hustling was in his blood, and with his older brother, and sister out the game now was his time to do his thing, and have the Henderson name cemented back in the hood. Sydney's own insecurities and lack of self-esteem found Kaylen carrying her. He was with her when she escaped from Cleverfield Mental Home, and he was with her now whilst she contemplated her next move. He knew Sydney loved Judas, and half believed he felt the same. He'd listened to their pillow talk, and heard them share their dreams, yet there was still something snaky about him, something he hadn't managed put his finger on until Sydney had innocently answered a much awaited phone call. Usually Kaylen confided in Shelly, and respected her advice. She was sincere in her opinions and held no judgment towards either the situation, or person in their chosen topic. But even Shelly wouldn't understand how Sydney's love for Judas could turn into deceit over night. She had to come clean. Sydney had to come, as clean, as it was ever going to get between the trio and the hidden three. "What you thinking about?" Brittany asked Sydney snapping her out of her thoughts. She watched as Sydney pulled her hair back into a pony tail, and narrowed her brows as if she was transfixing into someone else. Sydney arched her back to stretch, and then clicked her fingers like a grown man before taking a seat next to Shelly on the bed. "I wanna show you both something." She began, "Something that got me through a lot of tough nights in Cleverfield." Sydney reached under her bed, and Kaylen came back up. He pulled out a large plastic container on wheels, filled to the brim with albums of photos from their past. "Do you guys remember what happened that night?" Kaylen asked. He pointed at a colourful picture the girls had had taken at the Notting Hill carnival in 03. They each wore outrageous outfits, with funky colours that bared more skin than fabric, and around their necks hung whistles, and horns among their multicoloured beads. "You both said I was crazy, talking about taking Bradley out when we had the chance, and look what he did. They all lie, I'm the only one of em you can trust, to keep you safe, and make you rich." Kaylen caught Brittany's eye and winked. "When I was walking around that fucked up ward I wasn't feeling sorry for myself, I was plotting revenge, revenge for us all." He toned his voice, so it sounded husky and low. "I got Judas covered for the most part, he's weak. I know how to work him." Kaylen rubbed his hands together and slyly smiled. "I'll soon have access to his complete stash." "Hold on, hold on, nah... Let me get this right. You ain't really feeling your sister's man! You're just fucking him so you can jack him?" Brittany asked confused. She couldn't understand why Sydney was being so devious and cold. "Shut up Brittany, and get with the damn program! You've robbed plenty of guys before. What! You don't like sharing the bate?" Kaylen looked at her and teased. Brittany had seen that look before, and shut her mouth. "Look, fuck

Bradley, fuck Judas; fuck Naomi, and fuck Craig. I'm tired of people taking shit from us. There's money out there waiting to be made and Judas is gonna lead us to it. I might not be righted up here," he pointed to his head. "But I'm honest, and loyal unlike most men. "Believe Judas planned on leaving Naomi anyway. It was just fortunate that little old Sydney came along." Kaylen said passing the pictures around. "Take a good look at where we've come from, and then think about how much were gonna need to hold to make sure we never have to come back." He pressed so Shelly and Brittany got the point. "You're sounding a lot like your dad Syd, all that money shit your talking's got me hype, but...." Brittany pondered on her but, biting her bottom lip. Shelly merely glanced at the picture Sydney now held in her hands, and before she knew it her cheeks were soaked with tears. She remembered every hour of that day to the fullest. So much so that she still had the beads she'd worn that afternoon. There were 18 red beads, and 29 greens, 15 blues, and 14 yellows. She remembered so vividly because those beads had fallen off their thread, and scattered around her bedroom floor whilst Bradley pounded away on top of her for the very first time. Seeing her own innocent face, reminded Shelley of Special now. It was her duty to protect her daughter from men like Bradley, yet she had her living, stifled under his roof. Almost immediately she became struck with guilt. Was she no better than her father? What if Bradley had already been molesting Special, and like her mother, Special was scared, and ashamed to say? All the same it would only be a matter of time before Bradley turned on Special. Even sooner when Angela learned that she was financially fucked. Shelly replaced the photo she held with the instructions Judas had given them, and read the details to herself. "I'm sorry Britt, but I need this right now." Shelly wiped her fallen tears and said. Was Sydney getting in way over her head? She asked herself whilst going over the details again.

Chapter 19

Sydney's sudden episode had stirred some old feelings Naomi thought she'd buried with her past. Her sister's illness saw her through some uncompromising situations, yet no matter how Naomi tried to help Sydney's attitude towards her remained the same. The Nurses, and Doctor's at Cleverfield said Sydney had matured over the past year, she had been taking her medication daily, and her progress had been extremely positive. Still, Naomi had her doubts. She couldn't help but wonder if the sudden change in Sydney's behavior was because she was well aware that she'd be stuck in Cleverfield forever if she didn't comply with the rules. It was impossible for Naomi to forget the state her little sister was in when she'd arrived at the police station after being notified of her arrest. Sydney was dressed in the skimpiest outfit Naomi had ever seen, covered in bruises, and had been charged with indecent exposure, and disturbing the peace. Obviously tired from her ordeal Sydney lay on the cold concrete floor and whimpered like a child. She'd been missing for almost eight weeks, and even though Naomi had filled in a missing person's report the authorities said there wasn't much they could do seeing as Sydney was considered an adult at eighteen. "Cleverfield Mental Home is not a maternal unit Miss Henderson and it is out of respect for your father that I have secured a bed for Miss Henderson. But, the staff there will not treat her if she is with child." "Who else have you told about your sister's condition?" Dr Shaperio asked after Naomi had practically begged him to meet her at the police station. After their mother, Naomi had run out of people to call. "No one Dr Shaperio, you were the first person I thought to call." Naomi had said. Dr Shaperio used to be her family's private doctor, and her father's honorable friend. "Good, good. You do understand that Sydney will not be able to leave Cleverfield's grounds don't you Miss Henderson? Not even if yourself deems her sane enough to be signed out. I have to warn you umm..." The Doctor tried to recall her name. "Naomi," Naomi said rushing through the paperwork. "Yes Naomi, I must warn you that Cleverfield is a place the mentally disturbed are sent to when their families fear the worst. It is a last result to send a young lady like Sydney to such a place, and then there is your sister's current condition." Naomi remembered the doctor warn her of Cleverfield being more than just a spare bed. But it was an option other than to bring her home. The care home she currently resided in was discharging Sydney from their care, they claimed that they no longer had to be responsible for her at eighteen, nor did they have the time, or energy to accommodate a rebellious runaway. "If you sign this piece of paper Naomi you are signing away your sister's freedom, and labeling her insane." Dr Shaperio said clearly, to make sure

Naomi was fully aware of the choice was about to make She couldn't even look the Doctor as she scratched the admittance form with her pen. She'd thought long, and hard about the decision she just made. No more sleepless nights, no more anxiety, and no more sitting by the phone waiting for a call to tell her Sydney was dead. Naomi had watched Sydney lose a piece of her own mind each and every time she changed. It broke her heart to see her sister suffer within a body her mind couldn't control. There was no telling where Sydney would wake up next if she didn't get professional help. Naomi pulled her mobile phone out her purse, and scrolled through her contacts contemplated who she could call. Judas had assured her Sydney was well, but Naomi knew she'd eventually have to come up with an explanation for her sister's outburst. He hadn't even mentioned her pregnancy. He just said Sydney was in her room with her friends, and that he was tired and going to bed. It had almost slipped Naomi's mind that he owed her an explanation too. But what was playing on her mind wasn't something he'd done, but something she'd heard him say. Naomi strolled down the contacts in her phone book and decided on calling Samantha for some advice. "Hey Nay, what's up?" Samantha sang happily into the phone after answering on the first ring. "You alright?" She asked not hearing a reply on the other end. "Yeah I'm fine Sam. I'm just heading home. What you up to?" she replied. Naomi didn't even bother to put any enthusiasm in her voice. She was tired of pretending that she lived a faultless life, right now she needed a friend, and Samantha was the only person she'd carried with her from her past that knew her well enough to listen to her vent. "Look, Naomi, I know something's up. I seen your face all day at work, and I know you've got something on your mind." Samantha was right. It had been almost impossible for Naomi to get the words she'd over heard Judas say to Sydney that afternoon. She had just greeted her client and assisted her into her seat at her station when she remembered that she hadn't locked her desk draw. It was only Judas and Sydney in her office at the time, but when they left, it would be unsecured, with a bunch of light fingered employees and customers walking around. 'I never meant for this to happen and I sure as hell didn't ask for this baby.' Naomi didn't understand. She stood by the door of her office blinded by the frosted window for a few more seconds, but heard nothing. Not because she wasn't listening, but because she had zoned out. While doing her clients hair, she asked herself over, and over again, what Judas could have meant. She knew him to well, and the fact that he was confiding in Sydney, her sister, and not her, alarmed her. "HELLO!" Samantha shouted through the phone. "You still there Naomi?" "Huh? Oh Sam, I'm here, I'm here. Your right my minds been somewhere else. Look, I know it's late, but I seriously need someone to talk to and..." Naomi was desperate to get another opinion on what she'd heard. It had been eating her up all day. "Nay, say no more. Where are you?" "I'm just at Dalston Junction, you live in Haggerston right?" "Yeah girl same place, 18 Haggerston Estate. Just beep your horn when you get outside, and I'll come down stairs to get you." Samantha said sounding delighted to have company. Both women said their goodbyes and hung up. "Are you sure you wanna park that amount of gwap on the Estate?" Samantha raised her brow, and asked as Naomi got out her car in a parking bay below her flat. She folded her arms across her chest in an attempt to keep her body warm from the cold, and wore a warm, and inviting smile as Naomi walked towards her fighting the September breeze. "Yeah, it's fine. I just hope I ain't disturbing you guys, coming over this late." Naomi said while leaning in to give Samantha a hug. "What, please, I wish I had something better to do, or someone." Samantha joked, and both ladies laughed. She led Naomi up two, urine drenched, flights of stairs to a balcony on the third floor, of which her flat was at the end. Despite the distasteful look of the estate itself, Naomi was taken back when she finally had the opportunity to step inside Samantha's two bedroom home. Samantha had put in some serious work. She laid down quality wooden floor boards throughout the property, and decked it out in a chrome and black bachelor style décor, except for the odd cushion and vase. The kitchen was off the hook, it was like something straight out of a magazine. Naomi couldn't help but wonder if she was paying Samantha a little too well at Queens. "Have a seat girl, I got this wine from Cost Cutter over there, but it tastes just like the good stuff." Samantha rambled her way to the refrigerator. She opened the chilled Jacobs Creek bottle of wine, and began to pour a glass for Naomi and herself, then brought the glasses into the lounge. "Hello, earth to Naomi." Samantha waved her hand to catch Naomi's attention. Naomi hadn't even sipped her wine. She just sat, and stared at her glass as if all the answers to life were suppressed inside. "Sam, I'm sorry. I Just..." Naomi stopped and bit her lip, tears filled her eyes and she could no longer hold them in. "I'm not ready to deal with this right now." She broke down and cried.

"Oh honey its okay, what happened? Naomi talk to me!" Samantha pleaded, comforting Naomi with a gentle rubbing motion to her back. Naomi went on to tell Samantha how Judas had reacted when she'd confronted him about their financial matters, she told her how he'd brushed her off then finally about what she'd heard. "It just doesn't add up Sam, why would Judas say something like that?" Naomi asked, not noticing the change in Samantha's body language, or the guilty expression on her face. Samantha looked away from Naomi as if she were pondering whether or not she should disclose what she'd seen many times with her own eyes. She sat up, took a sip of her wine, and then placed her glass on a coaster on her glass coffee-table before she began. "I don't think Judas's playing around Nay, but I did hear something. I mean I've been hearing things, but it really isn't my place to say." Samantha blurted out after much deliberation in her mind. "You heard something, and you didn't come and tell me!" Naomi screeched it seemed as if everyone around her knew something that she didn't, but she hadn't expected this from her best friend. Samantha knew more than anyone how low Judas's indulgence in fast women and unprotected sex could bring Naomi when his shit came out. "I tried Naomi, but I didn't get the time. I tried to get at you today at Queen's, but you were handling something with Sydney, and then Essen and I got chatting, the day dragged on, and I completely forgot about Mariah's ass running her mouth." Samantha admitted. Both women sat silently for a moment or two. Both contemplated whether to share the personal thoughts of their mind. It seemed silly for them to be so cautious and hesitant towards each other, seeing as they had been here many times before. Naomi refused to believe that Judas would disrespect, or deceive her by bedding another woman again, but, like those times before she had to know. Taking Judas back would depend on the hardness of the blow. "What is it Sam? Who is she?" Naomi demanded to know. "I'm not sure if there is a she yet, I mean I think there is. "But you said you heard something today, right?" "Yeah, but I need more information than I've got before you go off the rails." Samantha stressed beginning to feel uncomfortable. She knew that once the cat had peeked out the bag it had to be set free. No one appreciated a half-hearted story, especially when it regarded a scorned woman and her man. Naomi wasn't going to let this go. "Sam, don't fuck with me like we ain't been tight from day one. If you know something, then you'd better say it, if it was you and Spider you wouldn't even have to ask me twice." Naomi pushed. "Damn, okay." Samantha held her hands ups. "But let me ask you this?" She then picked up her wine glass and downed the contents before beginning to pour herself another. "Have you felt the need to check Judas's phone lately? Is he sneaking around? Acting guilty and you can't think of a reason why?" "No!" Naomi replied. "Then it's probably nothing but the game." Samantha gulped her drink then smiled. "Why you grinning Sam, this is serious?" Naomi screamed becoming frustrated with Samantha's riddles. Samantha was indeed her best friend but it wasn't by mutual choice; Samantha was Naomi's only friend. In secondary school, Samantha Bramble was just another broke pupil in her class. It wasn't until she'd married Spider and became Samantha Clarke that the women bettered their acquaintance and began regularly crossing paths with her. Their friendship was enthusiastic when Spider was servicing the streets and bringing home plenty to put Samantha in the league of someone like Naomi. Since Spider's incarceration, Samantha had been a constant reminder to Naomi that she was dependent on her man. Now, looking at her surroundings, all of the charming décor and furniture Samantha had squashed into her tiny council flat looked tacky and cheap. She could definitely do without Samantha's sarcasm and patronizing implications seeing as the new life she'd built for herself and her boys was in the slums. "I know this is serious, Nay, I'm just saying..." said Samantha. "You're just saying what?" Naomi asked, contemplating backing her drink. "You know what, we've been here before. What would it matter if Judas was playing around and I told you I heard or saw something that I thought looked suspicious but I wasn't really sure?" "Why would it matter?" Samantha asked, placing her empty glass down and passing her eyes over Naomi's full glass. "It just would, Sam, this time is different," said Naomi. Putting her hands on her small bump, she watched the expression on Samantha's face change to delight. "Oh my God!" Samantha screamed, "shut up, are you pregnant?" Samantha excitedly threw her arms around Naomi's neck. "Look, I'm sorry. You're my girl, and I love you but I ain't trying to be tip-toeing around King Judas over my mouth. I'm always gonna have your back though," she said excitedly, letting go of Naomi. "I know but I need to know, Sam," said Naomi. She crossed her arms and walked around Samantha's coffee table, focusing her attention on a wall filled with pictures that Samantha had collected and put together of her, her husband and their twin boys. "Look, all I know is Mariah has been on some diva shit lately; coming in late, not coming in at all and recently she started to talk a lot of shit," Samantha began before Naomi interrupted her flow. "Tell me Judas isn't fucking someone where I work, not where I work?!" Naomi exclaimed, fighting back more tears. "Wait, Nay, that's nothing. I don't know if Judas is sleeping with Mariah, I just suspect. What I do know though is that Mariah is a tenant in your block and she has been for two years," said Samantha, proud that her investigating had been of significant use, "I overheard a customer ask her if she still stayed over at Bowma Tower. When she said yes, I called Melanie." "Who, Sideburns-Melanie?" Naomi asked as she wiped her eyes and cocked her head. Samantha rolled her eyes. "Anyway, Melanie's staying with her baby father, Chad, who's a tenant of yours. I could tell she'd didn't wanna say anything but she eventually slipped up. She said that a couple of tenants in the building had complained of the strong burning smell contently coming out of Mariah's apartment. You know Melanie just had a baby right? So she was like, Mariah needs to either put out the fire out or get out." "This is the first I'm hearing of this, why didn't she call me direct?" Naomi asked, clearly confused. "Listen, wait, that's not all!" Samantha hushed her, "she said she spoke to Judas about it plenty of times. In fact, after the last time she'd spoken to him about it, she hadn't seen him around yet his car would always be parked out front. She figured he must have been avoiding her. I can only imagine the hell she was going through with her floor always smoked out. She said the corridor was constantly filled with fog that snuck into her flat under the door." "I don't blame her for what she did next though," Samantha added as she poured herself another glass of wine, emptying the bottle into her glass while Naomi waited for her to continue. "I know it ain't funny but I couldn't help but laugh when she told me she took her pregnant ass down a flight of stairs and banged on the tramp's door with a rolling pin in one hand and a Dutch-pot lid in the other," Samantha paused, "she said Essen opened the door and there was a bunch of naked bitches up in there he was trying to hide." "Essen, huh?" Naomi repeated, uncrossing her arms and placing her hands on her hips. "Yeah, she couldn't see Mariah but she heard Judas's big mouth shouting orders from somewhere in the flat. There was a whole bunch of shit popping off in there that Melanie didn't understand but when she explained what she saw to me, I knew exactly what Judas was running from Mariah's flat. The smell, the smoke, the naked workers in masks and white powder; all that shit reminded me of when I first met Spider, and he set up a private kitchen in his Grandma's basement, turning cocaine into crack. The smell went straight to my chest the first time I walked into the closed room. We wore masks while he taught me his trade and on the odd occasion when we were pushed for time, I'd bring Tanya's older sister Rachel with me and we'd work naked. Spider said that was to make sure Rachel's shady ass didn't steal any off his shit." When Samantha was finished, Naomi stood shocked. She didn't know what to say. What Samantha had told her had slightly shaken her world. "I know it's a lot to take in, Nay, but that's the way it's going down," Samantha said apologetically. Samantha slightly regretted the fact that she had to be the one to the shed light. She knew the Naomi her friend was before she was Judas's Naomi and the Naomi she knew then would never let a man come between all she had worked and strived for. "What about Judas and Mariah?" Naomi wanted to know, thinking there was still a possibility that Judas and Mariah were getting sweaty under the sheets. It wouldn't be the first time Judas brought his work home. "Like I said, I don't know," Samantha replied, joining Naomi by the wall, "but real talk, Naomi, you need to open your eyes. I see the way you swan around like you never grew up in the hood and the streets wasn't your home. I know we're on different sides of the poverty line right now but I ain't lost my sight to see when a woman's being played. In my opinion, Judas ain't doing you right, but until you feel your suspicions luring you to my first set of questions, you gotta sit tight. Don't tell Judas nothing I just told you until we're 100%, understand?" "I hear you, Sam, and I appreciate you being real," Naomi replied, grateful for the support and guidance Samantha had given her despite her faults, "I just wish I knew what to do with what I know now." "What do you mean?" Samantha asked, looking at Naomi like she should know, "first thing first, that bitch Mariah has got to go," Samantha added before Kieran and Kareem came stumbling through the front door.

Chapter 20

Judas sat back in the lazy boy chair in the lounge, surrounded by his team, puffing on a joint. He reminisced back to a few nights ago when he had Sydney spread eagle on her hands and knees in that very same chair, him tugging on her curly hair, and arching his back while penetrated her from behind. "Now this is what a nigga wants to see when he gets outta jail," said Sticks as he rubbed his hands together and rose from his seat. Shelly, Sydney, and Brittany walked elegantly into the dimly lit hallway, looking like they were the convention's top prize. "Naomi's sister and her girls got body for real," Sticks added, ogling the girls as Judas got up to see them to the door. Their target that night was a crud young hustler named Smiley who was confirmed to be attending one of the biggest gambling attractions in the West End. Smiley would have at least over $100,000 with him in cash, just over half of what he owed Judas for a consignment agreement that had taken place between the two before Smiley snuck out of town. Judas knew this for sure because that was what was required as a down-payment per playing attendee. It had been eight months since Judas had heard from the little shit which meant he'd been in hiding and Judas hated a punk that hid. Now Smiley may have been gambling addict but he was no fool to the dangers of the game. He was one of the grimiest little niggas around the hood and he was going to the venue strapped with an entourage of stick up kids as grimy as they came. "Sydney, let me holler at you for a minute," Judas said, stopping just outside his closed apartment door. "Let me go see what this nigga wants," Sydney whispered before walking towards Judas, leaving Brittany and Shelly to wait for her by the elevator door. "What's up with Syd, Shell? I know it ain't just me. She's tripping right?" Brittany whispered to Shelly as they waited patiently for Sydney to come back, "I mean, it sounded like she's talking about fucking Judas up when the other day she was cursing me out and defending their affair." "What's up with all that, Shell, cos I know you know?" Brittany questioned. "What...! What you talking about Brittany?" Shelly tutted, breaking out her own thoughts of doubts, 'I'm the only one of 'em you can trust,' she remembered Sydney saying which was confusing because she could have sworn Sydney was referring to herself as a man. "You know what I mean, Shell, all of this," Brittany added, referring to their attire, "you know me, I'm down for whatever. I just hope Syd knows what she's getting us into." She thought back to the other night when she caught Sydney and Judas butt naked, fornicating in Naomi's bed. Sydney had bitten down on her bottom lip and let out short moans of pleasure. She had held an enthusiastic expression of satisfaction on her face while Judas watched her lustfully straddle him, locking her legs around his waist. 'Yeah, it just happened, my ass," Brittany snickered. She could have watched Judas and Sydney tease each other all night from the crack in the door in the shadows the apartment created by the moonlight. "This is careless, Syd... You know...Naomi's...gonna be back... soon," Judas panted as Sydney grinded her pantieless crouch on his hardness through his jeans. "This is wrong Syd... It's wrong," Judas moaned even through he didn't put up a fight. Brittany moved to the other side of the door whilst their body's intertwined on top of the sheet. She now spied on their lovemaking from the reflection in the mirror that hung tilted above the head of the bed. "Don't act like you don't want this right here," said Sydney, playing in the wetness between her legs. Judas was mesmerized; Sydney had him right where she wanted him at that moment and that was right there with her. Judas was shook, Brittany could tell. He kept trying to look towards the door but Sydney pushed him back down. "Come on, Judas, play with me," Sydney whispered, tugging on his jeans. She fumbled with his zipper, and freed him of his pants and boxer shorts. They kissed and groped each other while Brittany watched with wide eyes and opened mouth. The way Sydney rocked her hips above Judas's groin had Brittany bobbing her head to Sydney's imaginary, sensual beat. "Stop teasing me... let's do this," Judas said as he slapped Sydney's ass, holding his erection in his hand. "Let me see you stroke it for me," Sydney stood back and said, unbuttoning her shirt. "Come on, Syd, you know I hate it when you ask me to do that shit," Judas whined, though he couldn't help comply. Sydney watched as Judas stroked himself with a firm grip from his right hand whilst he rested the other around her waist. "You like that, huh?" Judas panted and reached up, grabbing a handful of Sydney's curly hair in his hand. He pulled her on top of him and tongue kissed her deep. Brittany never knew Sydney got it in like that. She didn't even talk about her rendezvous. Standing at the cracked doorway, Brittany couldn't tell whether it was Judas holding his swollen dick or Sydney gyrating her hips that had her wet between the thighs. Sydney rode Judas with passion; he moaned and groaned each time she rose and slid back down and then closed his eyes. He placed both hands around Sydney's waist and guided her spot where he wanted it to be. "Ummm, yes, Judassss," Sydney yelped. "Susssh...." Judas whispered out of breath. He pulled Sydney further towards him, placed one of his hands behind her neck and pulled her closer, pushing himself deeper inside her love. In the depth of the night and in the solitude of their four walls, Sydney and Judas's energy had taken Brittany to an x-rated state of her own. Every time Judas raised his hips, Sydney grinded down and when he hit her hard, she bounced him right back. Brittany had been so caught up in their love making that she hadn't noticed Sydney's eyes, wide open, watching her reflection as she watched Judas and hers. Sydney's eyes latched on to Brittany's but she kept on doing her thing. She then hopped up onto her feet and slammed her ass down into Judas's groin, throwing him off his game, causing him to stutter her name. "Sssydney, damn. Awww shit," Judas breathlessly let out. Brittany giggled at Judas's sock-less feet; his toes twitched and flicked like they were on fire. She couldn't help but bite her bottom lip and adjust the crouch of her knickers. Sydney was throwing down some ass. She moaned when Judas raised his crotch to meet her depth and it was then Brittany knew that Sydney wasn't Syd. Growing up next to the Hendersons had gained Brittany more knowledge of the family than she'd ever let on. She had heard all their visitors come and go which was how she'd overheard Dr. Shapiro detailing Sydney's state of mental health to her parents before he left. She knew about Sydney's diagnosis, the medication and the reason behind her being sent to Cleverfield. Either way, Sydney was her girl, she'd accepted Sydney for who she was and generally enjoyed hanging out with her inner personas from time to time. It wasn't their presence that had Brittany tripping, it was the fact that she was no longer able to tell them apart. She'd never forgotten the day Kaylen introduced himself to her, it was during their early teens. Brittany and Sydney were sitting outside the Hendersons' front door talking shit when Naomi came outside and cursed them both out for talking too loud. She had originally sent them outside when the family's lawyer arrived. Sydney was pissed as usual because she felt excluded from their discussion. Being the youngest of the Henderson household at thirteen, she wasn't considered old enough to listen in. "This is bullshit, Naomi! I understand that Daddy's dead so how come you all think that I won't understand what that man says?" Sydney shouted to her sister through the letter box after Naomi had closed the front door. "Forget all this, Syd, let's holler at Bradley," Brittany offered, pulling Sydney's arm. She had never seen her best friend filled with so much pain and sorrow. She led the way to Bradley's house on the other side of the street. "See how they treat me like a baby?" Sydney moaned pulling her long, curly mane back into a ponytail. Kaylen didn't like having Sydney's long hair in his face, it made him feel like a certified bitch. Lucky for him, Sydney looked the shit in anything she wore; she rocked the hell out of an Adidas tracksuit and always kept her Air Forces tight. "My mum doesn't wanna sell the house because she says it has got too many memories in it but how we gonna remember my dad if her and Naomi keep selling his shit?" He continued pacing the pavement whilst Brittany ran up the steps that led to Bradley's house and rang the bell. Kaylen had plenty of other friends he could hang out with on the other side of town but he considered Brittany to be his best friend. No one else would understand. "I hear you, Syd, but your family's always gonna see you as the baby. You're the youngest in your family and let's be honest, we're thirteen, we're kids," Brittany replied before a teenaged girl answered the door. Together, they bought a score bag of Tye and ended up in Brittany's bedroom for the rest of the afternoon. Brittany's parents were almost never home and because her mother smoked weed, they didn't have to worry about masking the smell. "How comes you act different when your hair is pulled back like that? Everything about you's different yet you're still the same person," Brittany had plucked up enough courage to ask Sydney when they were sprawled out on her bed, enjoying their high. "What'd you mean different?" Kaylen rolled on to his stomach and asked, placing his hands behind his head. "You act like a boy," Brittany replied, looking him dead in the eye. She swallowed hard when Sydney didn't reply. It was hard to read the expression on Sydney's face. Brittany wasn't blind to Sydney's frequent visits to the family's personal doctor and she'd heard Sydney during her episodes through her bedroom wall. "You don't need to pretend, Syd, I know you're sick and I wanna help." "Well you can't help because I'm not sick," said Kaylen, turning away from Brittany. His expression was dead serious and thuggish before he curled the corner of his mouth up into a devious grin. "Sydney ain't here with us anymore, Britt. Tonight it's just me and you." "I knew it, I knew it..." Brittany whispered gently, punching Kaylen in the arm then falling back onto the bed. Everything suddenly began to make sense. "I knew I wasn't crazy and there was something going on inside your head," Brittany said sitting up, "who are you and what's happening to Sydney while you're here?" she demanded to know. She was undoubtedly intrigued by the stranger but she had to hold down her girl. "I don' know," Kaylen chuckled, "but however you're thinking, I'm sure it doesn't work like that. I'm guessing Sydney's right here," he added as he pointed to his head, "she's just in the back if you know what I mean." "So you share the same body?" Brittany asked, feeling an awkwardness creep into the room. "Nah, I like to think of it as us sharing the same mind," Kaylen laughed, "I'm not a girl, Brittany. I'm a boy, you'll see the difference when I'm around," he said, flashing a mischievous grin. "Syd, you sure you're ready to do this?" Judas asked as he stood close to Sydney, paranoid that her friends were eating their words. Walking out of the apartment dressed up with her girls, Sydney's heart pounded rapidly when the realization of her new position in Judas' life began to take effect. She still wanted to love her sister but standing next to Judas, looking in his eyes and seeing his concern for her just couldn't compare. "I guess," she replied. "Alright, good, I need you to be focused tonight, Syd, really think about what you're doing. I know you and your girls know your way around town but the hood and people ain't the same. There's no telling what kind of muscle this motherfucker got with him tonight so I want you to take this just in case you need it." "Awww, and there I was thinking you didn't love me," Sydney teased him as she took the hard object wrapped in a hanky and placed it in her purse. This wasn't her first time handling a piece. "I'll take it because I don't want you to worry but I doubt there will be any need for drastic measures," she explained, "a man only keeps one muscle in attendance when he's around me," she joked but Judas didn't follow. "Look, let's just put in this work, get this dough, settle the score with Naomi and be out. I need you to be on point. understood?" Still tired from this afternoon, Sydney nodded, yes. "Don't nod, Syd, say yes," said Judas as he grabbed her arm. He wanted to hear loud and clear that Sydney understood what she and her girls had signed up to do. "Yes, I understand," Sydney replied as she pulled away before they became too close. Judas could feel Shelly and Brittany watching them so he caught on to Sydney's hesitance and discreetly pulled away. He then raised his head to Brittany and Shelly, leaving them in Sydney's care. "So what they saying? They ready?" Essen asked when Judas had returned to the apartment and resumed his place in his lazy boy chair. "Yeah man, they're straight," Judas replied. He poured himself a shot of Remy Martin and downed it, pondering whether he'd made the best decision for the team. His usual female workers would have rather tussled in the sheets than ventured into the streets but he treated them all the same. He was always building a relationship with the individual, be it physically or mentally, because he was a slave for the goods and the women of East London knew this well. Judas could never reject the temptation or the pleasures a beautiful woman could give. Most of the women on his team were at one time, before meeting Judas, financially fighting to survive. Judas gave them hope, there was no dark place a beautiful and intelligent woman could be that could have deterred him from his prey. He showed them an expensive trade, put them to work, coaching them into the game and in return, they thanked him by offering access to worship in the temple between their thighs. "Aye, Judas, listen to what Nugget done told us when you left the room," Sticks cut into Judas's thoughts. "What's that?" Judas asked, looking unfazed. "That white chick that rolls with Naomi's sister used to be Craig's main chick." "I thought it was her when they came through the door, wasn't sure until she started with the attitude," said Nugget. "Boy, please, how'd you know it was that white chick you saw Craig with and not another? They all look the same to me," Judas replied, though he had other things on his mind. "C'mon, man, I ain't stupid," Nugget tutted, "I seen them down Mackie Dee's in Bethnal Green. She was cursing out the man serving her at the drive through, I got a good look at the bitch. I'm surprised she didn't recognize the kid." "Well," Judas snapped his knuckles, "if Brittany doesn't know where Craig is, and what his sneaky ass is up to, she'll be in for a shock when he becomes her target." "You think she knows where he is?" Nugget asked Judas, leaning in to hear what he says. "Who cares?" Sticks said before Judas could answer. He jumped out his seat, stretched his back and took the floor. "You heard what my man said. If she doesn't, she's in for a crude awakening when they cross paths," he continued, pouring Jack Daniels into his empty cup. I know women like that Brittany, it's women like her that have us niggas filling up jails," Sticks then laughed, downing his drink and grabbing the bottle to refill his glass again. "Speaking of jail," he said, raising his glass, "this man here is the reason I'm standing before you all now. Essen, I owe you man!" Everybody except Essen laughed. "THEY CAN'T HOLD US!" Sticks shouted, spilling his drink, "they tried to lock me up on some bogus rape charges when we all know the hoe wanted all of this," he raved, holding his crutch. He continued entertaining his crew while Essen looked on in disgust. "I would have loved to see the look on Kenosha's face when her old man got popped. You all should have seen his face when he walked in on his baby girl snorting a line butt naked while I played in her ass," he continued, detailing the cause of his arrest. "How much do you bet our Brittany's a little freak?" Sticks asked Judas whose mind seemed to be elsewhere. "I don't know but I bet it won't be hard to find out," Judas replied. He couldn't help thinking about Sydney and her outburst that afternoon. Something wasn't right in the way she'd acted. The raving and ranting he could justify because of the circumstances but the wet hair and towel had him wondering if the illness Naomi said Sydney suffered from as a child existed anywhere other than in her head.

Chapter 21

Cee sat comfortably on the neatly made double bed in the penthouse suite of the Idris Hotel he'd checked into in Excel and counted his money while on the phone to his cousin Nathan in jail. "Nathan, Cuz, calm down! You and your boys are gonna be straight, I just got off the phone with your solicitor and he's hard at work trying to get you out of there but this new charge that has been put on you and your boys needs to be dealt with before he can do anything else," Cee told Nathan whilst he stacked the piles of fifty pound notes into piles of a thousand a piece. "Fuck Tennyson and Felt, Cuz," Nathan stressed, "I don't give a shit about them right now! I heard they done talked to the feds. Just concentrate on me, I ain't confessed to shit and I sure as hell ain't about to go down for killing a nigga I didn't kill," he said before the operator notified him he had one minute remaining of his call. "Look, just calm down and sit tight," Cee repeated again, "keep your head down and your ass in line. None of this would have even happened if you had come to me first instead of hollering at Judas to put you down," Cee finally admitted. He was still pissed that Judas had the audacity to hit him again. In fact, the first time Judas had jacked him for his product hurt the most. Cee was black and blue for days after the attack and Judas had even had the nerve to say that if Cee knew the fuckers that hit him, he and his team would be down with him if he wanted to hit them back. "I don't know how long I can take it in here, Cee, for real. I'm... I'm scared," Nathan broke down and sniffled into the phone. "I know, Nath, but you gotta be strong," Cee replied before the operator disconnected the call. He knew his cousin was in a bad way from what his lawyer had told him but hearing Nathan crying tore Cee apart. He'd fled his apartment in Southwold Estate and had been laying low, checking into different hotels on the other side of town. Like Nathan and his boys, Cee also grew up in South London but had moved to East London with his parents in his early teens. "The quicker I get the fuck up outta here, the better," Cee mumbled to himself as a reporter on the television discussed news of another killing in Hackney. An airy feeling came over him when the reporter stated that the victim was killed as a result of his daughter running wild in the streets. Though that wasn't the reporter's exact words, Cee had come to his own interpretation of the killer's reason for motive, judging by what he'd heard on the streets. If you were down with the community in the hood, the news only gave you what the evidence told. The people and the buildings told the real stories behind the reporter's exaggerated scripts and the newspaper's catchy headlines. Cee thought about his own problems, "I can't believe Judas hit me again! And this time, he had the nerve to set my cousin up to do the job," he vented to himself, "then there's Brittany. She talked a good game but when shit hit the fan, the bitch was ghost." His sister Jessica had told him that she'd been around the house, questioning his whereabouts and demanding dough. "Fat chance of you getting any of my shit, bitch!" Cee laughed, picking up his phone to make a call. He couldn't lie, it hurt that Brittany had proved to be as slimy as he'd heard her to be on the streets. He had real feeling for the girl and felt stupid because he believed that her feelings were mutual and they were on the same wave. Cee had fallen hard for Brittany, so hard that he'd been tailing her for the last couple of days. Maybe something had happened to her and that was why she was unable to receive his calls? Or what if Judas was holding her to make sure he got paid? Judas wasn't that cunning. Besides, he'd been his connect way before Cee got it together with Brittany. Cee only had to get Jessica to call a few hospitals to find out that Brittany had been treated at Whipps Cross on the night he was robbed and shot but that was all the receptionist would disclose. Cee wasn't stupid, he'd felt Brittany's extra weight and she knew he didn't want kids. Funny thing was though; he would have considered just the one with Brittany if it was her wish. He couldn't even blame Brittany for handling herself behind his back. The amount of times he had sat with her and laughed at the so called players sporting baby mothers, not knowing that their baby mothers were sporting them, was endless. It took him a while to admit it but it wasn't Brittany that was to blame, he fucked up by neglecting to notice that his woman had a heavy decision on her heart. He should have been there for her when she needed him but shit happens and he would have taken her back if he hadn't seen her coming out of an apartment he spotted Judas leave two days ago. Brittany had officially made it onto Cee's 'get back' list. He'd made a vow to himself that he'd deal with both Judas and Brittany for their betrayal before he left town; the only thing that could stop him was his death. "Hey, can I speak to Natasha please?" Cee asked after listening to the phone ring a number of times before the female, who regularly evaded his mind and dreams, picked up. "Yes, this is Natasha. How can I help you?" she asked in a sleepy, irate manner, as if Cee had interrupted her sleep. "Shit, I didn't even see the time, let me let you get back to sleep and I'll holla at you some other time..." he began, cursing himself for not being more considerate of the time. He was feeling this chick Natasha but he'd risked disrespecting her by calling her at 'booty-call-O'clock'. "By the way, it's Cee. I was just checking on you... you know, but Imma hit you back because it's late and I know you and your daughter must be asleep," Cee added before Natasha's soft voice soothed him through the phone. Cee knew getting involved with another woman wasn't the right move for him now but Natasha had him digging her from the moment they'd first met. Cee had raced out of his driveway and sped down the street from his intruders without the slightest twinge or pain to indicate he'd been shot. The adrenaline that pumped through his body when he'd jumped over his back fence and into his car hadn't let up until he'd stopped at a red light and caught his breath. As soon as he saw the blood, his right arm fell heavy and numb. He saw that he'd lost a fair amount of blood and applied pressure to his wound with his left hand until the traffic light's changed but the pain made it unbearable to drive. "Awww fuck..." he groaned out in pain as a burning sensation engulfed his right arm. In his haste, to escape, he'd left his phone in his apartment so he couldn't call his girlfriend but she should have been by his side. He'd been calling her all afternoon and evening and she hadn't returned any of his calls. "You okay in there?" Cee suddenly heard a woman say. He sat up straight, used his bloodstained hand to wipe the sweat from his face and, without thinking, turned to see the face of a woman tapping the window of his car. At that moment in time, Cee couldn't have cared less about stopping his car in the middle of the road. He turned away from the woman, holding his arm, then turned back alarmed when she threw open his car door. "Sir, I can help you, I'm a nurse!" she said, trying to get a better look at his arm. Her eyes glanced past the stack of bills and Clingfilm wrapped around product Cee had carelessly thrown into the front seat. "Can you drive?" she asked him while taking off her scarf and tying it tightly around his bleeding wound. Cee winced, "nah," he said, watching as the mysterious girl hurried back to her car. Still holding his arm, he sat back and breathed through the pain, watching through his rearview mirror as the woman parked her car at the end of the street, pulled something off her back seat and made her way back to him. "I'm gonna need you to get to the passenger's seat, you think you can do that?" she asked, standing between Cee and his car door. That's how Cee had imagined Natasha ever since he'd met her two weeks ago. 'What were the chances of me running into a nurse?' he asked himself while Natasha pondered to answer a question Cee had asked her a thousand times since they'd started speaking on the phone. "Okay but its only dinner right?" Natasha finally said to Cee's amazement as he'd expected her to say no. She hadn't mentioned the money and product she'd seen in the car but Cee was pretty sure that was part of the reason Natasha had been blowing him off. "Wow, I got an okay," Cee laughed as did Natasha down the phone, "I thought I was gonna have to shoot myself in the other arm to get a little bit of your time," he joked at his own expense. "Don't joke like that, Cee, I don't even wanna think about that night and I don't wanna see you getting shot again." Cee knew then that the feelings he'd felt for Natasha were mutual. He hadn't been able to stop thinking about the way she'd handled herself the night they'd met. She was calm and confident during her medical proceeding and hadn't once, up to this day, shown any signs of shock. She could have simply left him bleeding in the streets or did the most that a reasonable person would do and call 911 but she didn't. For some reason, Natasha had gone above and beyond and Cee refused to accept her kindness to him as just her doing her job. People rarely cared of people other than their own in the hood and never put themselves in unexplainable situations.

Chapter 22

Brittany held the small piece of paper that displayed hand-written instructions to their job outside the passenger side of Shelly's car window and set it alight. It immediately caught fire and turned to ash before Brittany let what was left go. Together, Brittany, Shelly and Sydney had memorized each and every word,until they were ready to put their plan of relieving Smiley of Judas's dough into action. Shelly rolled her car to a slow stop at the bottom of a quiet street next to Farringdon Station. It was 2:58am and there were still many people out loitering the streets. Neither of the girls had ever attended a gambling event so the atmosphere was a totally new experience for them all. They walked up the sidewalk, huddled together, and passed expensive auto-mobiles and their owners while loudly dressed people surrounded the exit of the event, exposing their wealth to the world. Sydney had overdone herself, pulling the numbers she had out of her wardrobe when she'd guessed the attire for the event. They each equally looked stunning; their bodies wrapped in free-flowing cocktail dresses, displaying their lady assets, best features and curves.

Two male passengers damn near tore their necks trying to check the trio out as they approached the brightly lit entrance of the club. Sydney let her hair flow straight down to her back while Shelly styled her amber, shoulder length cut into a bob. After searching through Sydney's largely expensive clothing collection, Brittany had picked out an oriental style dress that stopped just above her knee and pinned her hair up in a Japanese style pony-tail to complete her Middle Eastern look. With her long eyelashes and spray-tanned complexion, men went crazy for Brittany's oriental transformation so it was decided between them all that Brittany would be the perfect candidate to seduce Smiley into their trap. "This dress is ridiculously short, my ass is freezing and my tits look like they're gonna jump out my chest," Shelly complained whilst waiting in the line of club Elite. London's annual gambling convention was being held in one of the priciest venues in the West End so Judas must have had his work cut out getting his hands on not one but three tickets. "Shell, calm down," Sydney said, rubbing Shelly's shoulder, "I know you hate having your ass and tits on display but it's nice to show off what you got once in a while." Shelly used the club's tinted window at the side of her and looked herself over in her reflection. She then half heartily agreed. Brittany, and Sydney were both confident in their skin as neither of them wore the scars of shame and sexual abuse. Shelly never fussed over her figure and style; she wore jeans and Polo tops on a daily basis and rarely changed her attire for work. "You look amazing, Shelly." Brittany said, applying a final coat of a shimmering Chanel lip gloss to her lips, "but I don't have to tell you that." She used the tip of her gloss stick to point out a bunch of laid back dudes who checked them out on their way to the front of the line. "Brittany, no fucking about today, yeah," Sydney shot out of nowhere when the men had passed, entering the club. "What?" Brittany laughed, "just because you're all loved up don't mean we have to pass up on all this opportunity," she said as she extended her hands to the crowd around them. "I can guarantee you that we're gonna have that key in under an hour and then the night is ours, trust me," she winked before turning to the front of the queue. She was greeted by a huge, black, gap-toothed bouncer who licked his lips and rubbed his leather glove covered hands together as she stood before him in all her glory. "Good evening, ladies," the bouncer said, smiling a toothless grin. He chuckled to himself and rolled his eyes, watching Sydney and Brittany ruffle through their purses for their tickets. He'd secured the doors of numerous highly-demanded events and had come to find that it was mostly women who used fake I.D's or pretended they were someone who they wasn't on the guest-list, trying to get in for free. Barry started to sigh loudly and was about to ask the girls to step aside until he caught out the corner of his eye Shelly adjusting her underwear to sit discreetly under her dress. "Found them," Brittany said excitedly. Barry unhooked the rope separating the entrance of the club from the street and could only wonder what it would be like to feel the touch of either woman as they each walked past him cautiously into the club. Beyond the long mirrored corridor leading to the main conventional hall was out of this world. Once inside the grand hall, Sydney, Brittany and Shelly's mouths dropped at the elegance and beauty that surrounded them all. The hall was expensively decorated in red velvet wallpaper that opposed other leaf gold painted walls plus silk red and gold sheets that hung below a breathtaking painting of angels and demons above them. "This place is amazing," Brittany said, already scouting the hall for her next potential sponsor. "Yeah, it is, but listen," Sydney added as she pulled Brittany and Shelly aside. She remembered the look on Judas's face when he'd come to see them off and had long forgotten what she had taken from him and placed into her purse until she walked past the bouncer at the front of the club. She promised Judas she'd be on point tonight. It was her first chance to show him what she could do. Okay, she didn't have the confidence to take complete control over their first job but she profoundly anticipated their next. Her plan was to let Brittany do her gold-digging thing, throw some ass at Smiley if she had to, while she and Shelly located the safe-deposit key. "This is business, Britt, not pleasure. You can't take any of these ballers home with you tonight but I ain't saying you can't have some fun. Remember why we're here and what we've come to do," Sydney continued, seeing Shelly slipping into her shell, "try keeping your stuff in your knickers tonight, okay? That's all I'm saying." "Yeah, yeah.... Business first, I know," Brittany rolled her eyes before taking off towards the bar and giving five to a girl that she rolled with around the way. "I'm scared, Syd, and that's not even the worst part. While I'm here fucking around with you and Brittany, Special's at home, locked in the basement, probably wondering where the fuck I am," Shelly sighed when Sydney asked her, if she was alright with what they'd planned to go down. "I may not be the perfect catch like you and Brittany but I'm gonna be cool working from the back. I need this money, Syd, I need it bad. Special's growing up and the other day, she said she felt trapped," she admitted, "being here and knowing what I'm about to take part in scares the hell outta me, yeah, but what scares me more is the thought of Bradley, that sick bastard, touching my baby." Sydney swallowed hard, listening to Shelly speak about her painful home life before they approached Brittany at the bar. They caught up to her just as she was hugging her girlfriend good-bye after hustling her man and his boys for three drinks. "So, have either of you thought about how we're gonna find this Smiley?" Shelly changed the subject and asked once she'd reached the bar. Brittany handed her a champagne flute while Sydney, against her own warning, had been distracted by a gentleman whose face Shelly hadn't managed to see. "I don't know but we're at the bar and the nigga's got to drink so maybe he'll come to us," Brittany said, hoisting herself onto a stool. Sydney pushed through the crowded hall, almost reaching the bar, when she walked right into the chest of a face from her past. "Aaron!" Sydney screamed, almost deafening the tall, muscular man who'd kept her on her feet. She embraced him tightly and he held her close, burying his nose in her hair. "You missed me, huh?" Aaron asked in his deep, rugged voice. He drew away from Sydney and used his finger to push her hair out of her face. For two years, he'd rehearsed what he'd say to her if she walked back into his life and now that they were face to face, he had nothing. Brittany and Shelly watched from the bar as Aaron and Sydney played catch up and reacquainted themselves. They looked at each other and couldn't help but fall out laughing. "And the bitch had the cheek to tell moi to keep my knickers on," Brittany snapped. Shelly ordered another drink. "Can I get a Jack Daniels on the rocks?" she shouted over the music. People flooded through the double entrance doors, filling the hall, shaking hands, and flashing their jewels. Shelly had just paid for her drink and taken a sip when a weighty light-skinned brother and his entourage caught her eye. "How much you wanna bet that's our guy?" Shelly nudged Brittany discreetly, drawing her attention to the man. "What, him?" Brittany giggled, tipsy from the champagne that had put her over the limit after her drinks at the apartments, "if he's Smiley then it's a wrap. Let me go over there and get this over with," she added, picking her purse up from the bar. She pulled out her gloss and reapplied a fresh coat before sliding off her stool to meet their potential target with a devilish smile. She watched as he shared a few words with a waiter and anticipated the moment their eyes met across the jam-packed hall. He pointed to the VIP area and pushed a few notes in the waiter's waiting hand before following the heat from Brittany's stare into her eyes. He smiled. "Tell me you saw that?" Brittany grabbed Shelly and asked, stumbling back onto her stool. "Please tell me you saw what I just saw?" she said again. Shelly had seen what Brittany had seen and now she wished she hadn't been so bold as to point him out as their man. He had a 6 inch scar on his face that left him with a permanent smile. Somebody had cut his face from one cheek bone to the other, painfully splitting the corners of his lips. It looked as though he'd been through some extent of surgery and given up because the scars spoke for themselves. "Excuse me," a small Indian man said, tapping on Brittany's shoulder, scaring her half to death. Both she and Shelly turned around startled, neither one saying a word whilst the man continued his speech. "Sorry if I've disturbed you two beautiful ladies but my boss over there," he pointed to an area in the darkest corner of the VIP section where their suspected target had rested, "well, he has requested your company and would be delighted if you would accept his invitation to join him, at his expense of course." "Game time," Brittany whispered to Shelly. She backed away from her stool, fixed her dress and took the small man's hand in her own. "Nice to meet you...Umm...?" she waited for an introduction. "Herb," the Indian man shook her hand and replied. "Herb, huh! Well, um, Herb, me and my girl would love to join your boss at his expense but we're kinda waiting on our friend over there," she explained, pointing to Sydney who just so happened to look her way. Aaron also caught a glimpse of the Indian man stretching his neck in his direction. "Look, walk with me," Herb said, leading Brittany and Shelly to follow him through the crowd, "I'm gonna be honest with you lovely ladies, me and my boys are gonna be throwing a lot of money on the tables tonight and one of you angels might get lucky." Shelly rolled her eyes. "My boss is a well-respected man around these parts, wait until you see his poker face, it's shocking," Herb laughed as security granted them access in the VIP suite. *** "So how long have you been back in town?" Aaron asked Sydney after an uncomfortable silence. "Just a few months now," Sydney lied. She knew that Aaron would be offended seeing as she hadn't been in contact since she'd left him two years before. It wasn't that she hadn't wanted to see him, she'd thought about him plenty times whilst she was in Cleverfield but she couldn't bring herself to face him. "What happened to you, Syd? When you left, I asked a few of your friends where you were staying but no one knew where you were. You just vanished and Shelly and Brittany avoided me like I had the plague," Aaron painfully explained. Sydney remembered she'd been arrested during her last year of college but she couldn't remember the events that had caused her to be detained. She'd spent twenty-four hours in a holding cell before she drifted off to sleep. When she awoke, she discovered that she had been admitted to The Cleverfield Mental Clinic and later discovered that Naomi had sighed the paper work for her admittance and was funding the necessary fees. "I told you I was gonna stay with family outta town, didn't I?" she lied again. "Sydney, don't patronize me. As far as I was concerned, your family was here. What happened between us? Were things that bad that you had to leave?" Aaron wanted answers and he was demanding them now. "I thought we were planning to go to Uni together. What happened to you studying law? We damn near signed up at the same time and I only signed up because of you. I worked my ass off so I could afford for us to live on campus," Aaron said in dismay. All Sydney talked about during college was studying Law. She didn't want to be a lawyer, she wanted to join the police force and work her way up to detective. She reckoned if she could just get her hands on her father's case, she could uncover the culprit responsible for his death. "Aaron, I..." she paused. She really didn't know what to say. She only vaguely remembered the time they had spent together in college but she'd never forgotten the life they'd made. "SHIT!" Sydney said out loud. Looking past Aaron, she spotted Shelly and Brittany attracting the attention of a strange Indian man. "What?" Aaron asked, clearly annoyed. Once again, Sydney had put their relationship on the back burner. He turned around and followed her eyes. "Do you know that guy?" he asked after returning a respectful nod to the beady-eyed Indian man. "Nah, I don't know him but I'd better get back over there. You remember how those two get when I'm gone too long," Sydney laughed, desperately trying to change the subject but Aaron wasn't laughing. He just stared at Sydney, searching her face for the answers to the questions he'd waited so long to ask. "Aaron, I know you want an explanation but right here, right now isn't the time," Sydney said, sensing Aaron getting upset, "I wanna apologize for the pain I caused you. I know it was a shock when I left but..." "A shock," Aaron cut in, "Sydney, being shocked is an understatement. The love of my life disappeared without as much as a note. You've been gone for two years, Sydney." he said, now fuming. He hadn't noticed the volume in his voice had risen. "I was in love with you, Syd, I still am," he admitted, causing a scene. The space around Sydney began to close in on her as she listened to Aaron and excused by passers when they barged her on their way to the bar. The crowd was moving at such a pace that

Sydney had long lost sight of her girls. "Look, I didn't mean to ruin your night, Syd." Aaron calmly added, reaching for Sydney's hand. He was crushed. All the memories and pain he'd spent the best part of two years trying to rid his heart of had come flooding back in the little time he and Sydney spoke. He looked at Sydney, who was busy looking over his shoulder at her friends. "I guess I never stopped loving you. Seeing you tonight just brought back so many feeling, I can't explain," he continued, "I missed you." Sydney tip-toed and looked over Aaron's shoulder again. Brittany and Shelly were gone. "I never stopped loving you either, Aaron," she said, gently pulling away from his grip. The past they once shared was sacred and dear to them both but while Aaron deserved an explanation regarding her disappearance and departure from his life, Sydney thought the past was best left where it was. "Aaron, I've gotta go! Stick around and I'll catch up with you later," Sydney said promisingly before slipping into the moving crowd. Aaron nodded in approval and watched as Sydney barged her way through the hall. He was supposed to be celebrating his graduation with a group of friends from medical school but bumping into Sydney had left him disorientated and drained. He cleared his throat and straightened his clothes before returning to his table to rejoin his peers. He looked left and right, as if he were crossing the road, and scoped out his surroundings before pulling his wedding band out of his shirt pocket and placing it curely back on his hand.

Chapter 23

"I told you fucking with those dickheads would get you hurt. You're lucky I found your stupid ass when I did or I'd be explaining a lot more than your bumps and bruises to Mum," Kieran said as he lay on his bed on his side of the bedroom he shared with his twin brother Kareem. The odd wince Kareem let out every now and then was a sure sign that the boys he'd been jumped by meant business and wanted their message to be heard. "Yeah, well, this wouldn't have even happened if you'd just rolled with us," Kareem rolled over and groaned. "Why? So I could get my ass beat like you?" Kieran smiled. Naturally he was pissed that his brother had received a beat down and he hadn't been there to have his back but a small part of him hoped that this beating would be a lesson to Kareem. The boys that lived on their Estate had been hounding them for weeks now, trying to get them to join their gang. Kieran wasn't down with all that street jargon but Kareem was with it all the way. He was a proud son of an ex-hustler whose name was a legend around the way. "No, for respect," Kareem replied as he pulled a basin out from under his bed and spat out blood, "we'd be making crazy money running with the H-Boy's. I don't know if you've noticed but I'm craving a new pair of kicks every week and the cheque Mum brings home from the salon every month just ain't gonna stretch to that. I'm trying to get in with the big boys right now and if you knew what was good for you, you'd get in while their offering you a spot," Kareem informed his brother before the painkillers he'd taken kicked in and he drifted off to sleep.

Chapter 24

"If you'd like to follow me, Sir, I'll escort you and your party to our VIP section where your table awaits as well as your complementary bottle champagne," a half-hunched waiter rushed to inform the leader of an entourage that had turned heads upon their entrance of the prodigal venue Elite. Joshua Cruz had built quite a reputation for himself in the gambling industry, so much so that he'd attracted the attention of other wealthy gamblers who loafed the opportunity to beat him at a simple game of blackjack. "That's what I'm talking about, show me where it's at," Smiley answered, scouting the area. He wanted to see everything in the venue without being seen. "Right this way, Sir," the waiter led the way and as fast as he could, he escorted Smiley and his men to a large table at the back of the VIP section. He then quickly disappeared. The table could seat at least ten people and for anyone who just wanted to sit back and watch the show, there was a large black leather sofa that sat opposite a large glass window looking out into the main hall of the event. "I don't know about you but I need a girl on my arm while I'm turning over them cards," Smiley joked to no one in particular in his crowd. "I hear you, boss," a small Indian man said, rubbing his hands together as if he were trying to keep them warm, "want me to bring you the finest?" "Yeah, you do that, Herb," Smiley replied, looking out unto the grand hall. There was a lot of competition in the house tonight, like the Costello brothers from East Ham and Raider from Stamford Hill. These dudes were known as 'limitless gamblers' but that didn't discourage Smiley in the slightest. He watched as his boys got comfortable in their seats and began filling their glasses with champagne. Tonight, he was rolling with a new clique. They were all young and reckless but their loyalty to him was more valuable than their age. Smiley was undoubtedly the boss and they had no objections of change. "Man, I can't believe I'm chilling in the VIP and sipping on champs in Elite," Gattie, a thin, dark-skinned boy giddily shouted above the booming music. He sat on the corner sofa with a champagne glass in his right hand, staring down in amazement as his left hand slowly guided a red headed females head up and down in-between his crotch. Smiley smiled despite the disfigurement of his face. "You better believe it and you better enjoy it while it's lasts," he replied, looking back at his young warrior as Herb headed his way. "Man, we gonna be throwing it down tonight, tell 'em, boss," Herb excitedly ranted in his native accent and presented two drop dead gorgeous women before Smiley and his crew. "I'm glad you ladies decided to join us," Smiley said, handing each of the women a sparkle-filled glass. Both of them were equally beautiful but he'd had his eyes on the Asian looking chick with the gold tooth and ocean blue eyes.

They engaged in idle conversation and had yet to exchange names when they were boorishly interrupted by the commotion at the VIP door. "If I were you, I'd take your motherfucking hands off my arm before I break it," a stunning female shouted at the bouncers after they'd repeatedly informed her that, without a pass, she wasn't getting close enough to the door to get a peek. "My girls are right there!" she pointed and tried to claw herself past the two hostile, obese men. "That your girl?" Smiley laughed and asked the two women in front of him as the bold but beautiful young lady continued to curse. Embarrassed, they nodded, sipping their drinks and hiding smiles behind their tilted glasses. Smiley loved a woman with a bit of fight, especially one who reckoned she could break the arm of an ex-heavyweight champion. "What's up, Darren? My girl giving you trouble?" Smiley pounded the bouncer that had a hold of the troublesome woman and greeted him like an old friend. Darren's jaw dropped and he immediately let the female go, apologizing for his mistake. He claimed, in his defense, that it was getting harder and harder to determine the real women from groupies. "Shall we...?" Smiley held his arm out for the lovely woman to take. "Thank you," she accepted even though she continued to glare at the bouncer with disgust. "I'll make sure she behaves for the rest of the night," Smiley turned and said to Darren before escorting the female past the rope. The feisty woman he sported on his arm was a goddess compared to her willing blue-eyed, gold-toothed friend. "I can't believe you bitches left me like that," Sydney said as soon as she pulled out a chair at the table. "Well, unlike some of us, we're taking care of business and if you hadn't noticed, scar face over there is our target," Brittany said point blankly. "What the fuck is wrong with you, Brittany?" Sydney stepped forward and asked, "you see his boys over there. I suggest you mind how loud you speak before business takes care of us." With that said, Sydney sat down and pulled her Victoria Secrets lip gloss out her purse, re-applying a fresh coat. Aaron had thrown her off her game and now she had an uneasy feeling in her stomach, like things weren't going to go to plan. She glared up at Smiley as he sat at the far end of the table but he had a direct view of both everything and everyone in the room. He looked over in the girl's direction a few times but any time either of them made eye contact with him, he turned away. Taking a grievous loss at an illegal gambling spot in East London had left him bankrupt and scar-faced. Smiley had teamed up with a devious bombshell named Cindy and together they hit the gambling world hard. Cindy, with her blue eyes and pale skin, was a significant distraction amongst his opponents in the game. She played the flirtatious girlfriend while he played the jealous boyfriend who'd get upset when she congratulated other players in the game. Smiley's opponents, either shaken or amused by their eruptions, paid more attention to the couple than they did the actual game. Smiley and Cindy always came out on top. Well, they would have, if Cindy hadn't been addicted to crack. Her addiction made her careless and eventually caused them to get caught. "You think this is funny, you little shit?" Smiley's opponent had sneered at him around the table when he'd suspected that he'd been a victim of Smiley and Cindy's card-swapping scam. "Oh, I'm sorry, man. I don't know what you're talking about," Smiley laughed him off as not to cause suspicion amongst the other players, "you snooze you lose now get the fuck outta here," Smiley continued to laugh as the man removed himself from the game. "I'll give you something to smile about," Smiley's defeated opponent mumbled, humiliated, and embarrassed by his loss. He spun around without time for a reaction and lunged across the table with a 7inch blade drawn, slashinh Smiley clean across his face. "Smile, laughing boy!" the man screamed whilst being restrained to the table by the surrounding males at the scene, "smile!" he screamed again. Smiley had fallen to the floor, wailing and gasping for air. His mouth had been slit open from corner to corner, and he bled from cheek to cheek. That treacherous attack left him disfigured for life; he'd lost his pretty boy looks and with it his cocky attitude towards the game. Loose women were a matter of the past now for Smiley but his reputation kept them a constant flow. Since then, no woman had so much as looked at him without gasping or felt his touch without flinching or pulling away. From across the table, Smiley watched the pretty woman who'd accepted his arm apply her lip gloss and anticipated their next physical encounter. Her friends were okay but neither of them compared to their friend who kept on glancing his way. "Please tell me why we're just sitting around watching these fools get drunk," Shelly said under her breath. All she wanted to do was get the money and get out. Smiley's boys were starting to get bored with their groupies and their lustful eyes had begun to turn to them. "What's happening?"

Sydney finally asked Brittany. She was becoming inpatient and she could see that Shelly was getting nervous being around so many randy males. "This is a piece of cake, just give my opening," Brittany slurred. "So you got this right?" Sydney asked, coming closer to hear the answer. "What did I just say?" Brittany rolled her eyes. "Ok, whatever," Sydney shrugged. It honestly didn't matter to her who got the deposit key, she just wanted to go home. Here she was, risking her life for a man who was scared to devote himself to her when the love of her life was in the same building, willingly putting his heart in her hands. For the next hour and a half, Smiley kept a steady flow of champagne and other spirits coming to the table. Then, at quarter to three, a waiter brought an unopened bottle and two glasses towards Sydney, along with a folded napkin letting her know that it was a complimentary gift from their host. "What's that, Syd?" Brittany asked, grabbing the napkin out of her hand and opening it. Inside was a room key and a note that read: Call a taxi for your friends and join me in 15. The District Avenue Hotel. "How fucking delightful," Brittany barked and kissed her teeth. She looked over at Smiley and his companions as they guzzled down champagne and surrounded themselves with their winnings. "Come on Shell, I'm gone. I told you we shouldn't even have come," Brittany drunkenly spat and bumped into a few chairs as she got up to leave, "get a fucking taxi.....Ha! We drove, motherfucker," she slurred, slipping back into her seat. Brittany hadn't declined a single drink since she'd got out Shelley's car and now she could barely stand. Shelly shook her head in embarrassment whilst Sydney bit down on her bottom lip. 'Think, think, think,' she thought as she watched Smiley re-fill his empty glass. She smiled at him when he looked up and, this time, he smiled back. "Well, Syd, I guess it just isn't my world anymore," Brittany drunkenly slurred as Sydney and Shelly struggled to sober her up in the back seat of Shelly's car, "I don't blame him though. Who did we think we were kidding, dressed up like a couple of mini yous," Brittany added before she passed out, her head slightly tilted to the side, and drooling as she snoozed. "I can't believe this shit," Sydney shouted, pounding the backseat, "I turn my back for a couple of minutes, and you let Brittany drink herself under the table." "ME!" Shelly crocked her head and streaked, looking at Sydney like she'd gone mad, "I know you ain't trying to put this on me." "I came out with you despite my doubts remember, Mrs. no fucking about tonight, this is business and not pleasure, all that shit. I didn't get on to you when you stalled shit, talking to Aaron, and not once did I see you pulling the bottle out of Brittany's hand besides to pour yourself another glass," Shelly spat. She climbed out the backseat, slammed the door shut, opened the driver's door and slummed down in her chair. "It could have been either one of us with that napkin and door key," she calmly said to Sydney, what, did you just expect Brittany to go in there blind without even looking at the nigga? I ain't never got down like Brittany but even I know the game don't work like that. We should have known that we wouldn't just get to pick which one of us retrieved the deposit key from Smiley, we should have contemplated a plan each." "Well, I've got nothing," Sydney replied, resentfully looking at Brittany's reflection in the rear-view mirror, "and I know you ain't either so we might as well get the hell out of here and head home.". "HEAD HOME!" Shelly raised her voice, stirring Brittany slightly out her sleep, "I lock my daughter up in a basement for eleven hours a day, I tell you she told me she feels trapped and now you're telling me those seven hours and fifty-four minutes I've left her imprisoned alone has been in vain?" "I'm not saying that, Shelly, but I don't know what to do!" Sydney sighed, feeling defeated and almost in tears, "we all got different skills, why do you think I told you to holler at Brittany when I gave you the latest on Judas and told you what was up? I've known Brittany all my life and if anyone could pull something like this off, it's her." Without Brittany's advice or guidance, she was screwed. Only Brittany had proved to have the courage to seduce and manipulate a mogul like Joshua Cruz. "See, that's why I keep telling you to watch CSI on channel five," Brittany muttered in her sleep, "you put a few drops of Ortiz eyes-drops on your nipples and watch that fool knock himself out," she mumbled as she stirred before getting comfortable and returned to her sleep. Sydney hadn't heard what Brittany had drunkenly slurred in her sleep, she'd left Shelly when she'd admitted her defeat and her persona was replaced with Lashay. Lashay reached behind her seat and pulled Brittany's purse off the backseat. She pulled out the half-empty bottle of Ortiz eye drops, opened the nozzle and poured the remaining contents onto the palms of her hands. "Here goes nothing," she said, reaching under her bra and smothering her breasts with the clear solution as Brittany had advised. It had been a long time since Lashay had felt the need to interrupt Sydney's conscience with her presence, usually she ventured out while Sydney was asleep, but Kaylen hadn't allowed her to sit back and have them at a loss. "This shit better work or I swear I'm gonna kill Brittany," she mumbled, shaking her head as she grabbed her purse. She stepped out the car, leaving Shelly dumb folded and speechless as she led her ass across the road towards the entrance of the District Avenue Hotel.

Chapter 25

Oakland Due Avenue was asleep when Shelly dropped Sydney off at the entrance of her apartment building, as was Brittany in the backseat. Lashay stepped out of Shelly's Micra at the exact same time the lights out in the streets turned off. She grabbed Sydney's purse off the dashboard, closed her door quietly, walked around the front of the car and leaned through Shelly's window. "I can't believe you pulled that shit off tonight," Shelly high-fived Sydney. She then pulled a duffel bag from under her seat and passed it to her through her window. "And I still can't believe that shit Brittany said in her sleep worked," Lashay replied, taking the bag from Shelly and resting it on her shoulder. They›d more than excelled in their task and Lashay was just itching to show Judas how Sydney and her girls had come through. Kaylen had congratulated her by stripping and robbing Smiley blind while he was passed out. He jacked Smiley's jewelry for himself and five grand in cash for Lashay. "I'll get Syd to holler at you in the morning," Lashay spoke to Shelly. She walked bare footed to the apartment building entrance and greeted Ricardo, the sixty-two year old Spanish concierge, as she walked past the front desk towards the elevator and waited. Lashay had listened in as Kaylen manipulated Judas' decision to put Sydney on and had begged him to let her play a part. She hadn't stretched her bones in a long time and was growing tired of being left in the dark. At 24, Lashay was the oldest of the three and had been with Sydney from the very start. She considered herself to be a diva and it was those controlling habits and selfish ways that had Sydney and the others shipped off and locked up in Cleverfield at 18. It was guilt that kept Lashay at a distance. She'd exposed their existence and had them under clinical supervision for years. Walking Sydney into the elevator, Lashay pressed the button for the 19th floor and left Sydney alone. Sydney was exhausted. She held onto the elevator railing and stared at her reflection in the mirror in front of her. The $364.00 Prada dress she wore was crumpled at the waist and the right strap had been torn out of place. Smudged mascara stained her face whilst her freshly pressed hair stuck up out of place. She looked like a whore, "I know I don't usually say this often but thank you," she said to her reflection and could have sworn it winked back. She struggled to put the remaining pieces of the night together. All she remembered was getting into Shelly's car after leaving Elite but she couldn't remember how she'd ended up back home. She looked like a hot mess, bare-footed with a duffel bag on her shoulder, her shoes and purse in her hands with an uncomfortable burning sensation on her breasts. She had to give her alter egos their props though; when she needed them the most, they always came through. Juggling her shoes, Sydney searched the contents of her purse for her door key. She bypassed Judas' conscience and thought herself lucky she didn't have to use it. "I gotta remember to hide this," she spoke softly to herself as she put her key in the lock and opened the apartment door. Sydney had no intention of committing murder but she couldn't speak for the others. She hurried into the apartment and threw down her shoes, just about making it to her room when the lights flickered on and Judas cleared his.

Chapter 26

Naomi pulled open her glove compartment and fumbled through her usual car litter, searching for her bible before sitting upright in her seat and taking a deep breath. She felt hypocritical and fake, sitting parked outside St. Anders Church of England, nine years since the last time she'd shamefully sat in the pews. Keyshia Cole's 'Falling Out' blared from her 5-disc car sound system and by the time the chorus repeated itself after the second verse, Naomi was singing along as if she'd written the song and owned all its rights. "Sometimes I feel like there's no getting through to you, like you don't appreciate all that I do. You gotta tell me that you want me to stay. Don't turn and walk away," she continued to sing along, not caring if she was in tune. The drive from Oakland Dew Avenue to Stamford Hill in her old stomping grounds was what usually pushed church out of her mind but today the trip had been pleasant and smooth. Naomi had enjoyed the fresh air and appreciated the free time she had to clear her mind. "How did we end up being this way? What are we gonna doooo?" she sang with Keyshia who seemed to be singing from her own heart.

Naomi left her apartment at 8:15 to arrive at 10am, just in time for St. Andrews' Sunday morning service. It was agony trying to get a seat up front in the pews in St. Andrew's as everyone felt the need to be close to Pastor Kelvin. "Hello, are you listing?" he asked the congregation when he'd made a valid point and wanted testimony that he held their attention. "Hi," they'd all say in unison. It was a strange thing for a pastor to make a habit but it worked every time. Naomi smiled thinking about all the creative methods he used to explain God's message amongst his people. "Okay, here goes," Naomi said to herself, turning off her car sound system and unbuckling her seat belt. She anticipated today's blessing as she electronically locked her car and paced up the church steps in her 6inch Jimmy Choo's. Unlike the other church goers, in their cotton outfits, straw hats, and comfy shoes, Naomi was diva styled. She clutched her bible in her right hand and pushed open the church doors with the other. It was like walking into a temple; the strong smell of Frankincense took over her sense of smell and people bent down on their knees whilst a small group of elderly people handed out the reading booklet containing the pastor's readings and hymns for the day. "Excuse me, please." Naomi bent and whispered to a small, elderly woman, who had taken up an additional seat in the pew with her bag. She was in such a hurry to get settled that she hadn't yet recognized the elderly woman as an old family friend. "Naomi Henderson! Well I never," the frail Caribbean woman abbreviated Naomi's full name, "God has been waiting for you child, welcome back!" the woman continued and scooted closer, resting her arm on Naomi's strapless Louis Vuitton clutch. Naomi shifted to the left. It had taken her a minute or two before she could place the woman's face with a name. "Mrs. Hawker?" Naomi asked hesitantly, awaiting the old woman's response. She was elated to be re-acquainted with her childhood neighbor, a woman who played a fair hand in raising her when her mother was strung out on the streets. "My, my, child, you have grown up beautifully," the old woman smiled, playfully grabbing Naomi by the chin. She admired Naomi's physical appearance, no doubt comparing it to how she remembered her in the past. Today Naomi was all natural; no make-up, no hair extensions and no acrylic nails. At 29, Naomi was a stunning chocolate brown woman. Like her sister Sydney, she also sheared the same large brown eyes which they inherited from their father along with their dimples that gave them away as siblings all the time. Naomi was one shade darker than Sydney and although her hair looked immaculate in her short Victoria Beckham style, Sydney always had what was considered "good hair." "Thank you," Naomi mouthed, seeing as the service had begun. She sat back in her seat and quietly asked God for forgiveness. Something told her that she may need it in the upcoming months. The pastor conducted an uplifting and motivating service that almost had Naomi in tears. He spoke to her without calling her name and when he asked people from the congregation to come forward to receive a prayer, Naomi was first in line. The service had only suppressed the surface of Naomi's pain. There were still so many unanswered questions that needed to be explained and Naomi refused to go home to be met with more lies. Instead, she searched the church for Mrs. Hawker after the service and told her -without taking no for an answer- she was driving her home. She felt like a little girl again, waiting in the small lobby of the church whilst Mrs. Hawker and some other church goers blessed each other with warm wishes before they departed for their Sunday lunch. The Hendersons were active members of the congregation when her father was alive but after the rumors and allegations made against him hit the news, Naomi barely had the nerve to look the older folk in their faces. "Let it all out, baby," Mrs. Hawker sincerely said when Naomi couldn't hold in the tears anymore. She knew pregnancy would affect her emotions but she hadn't expected to feel so tired and withdrawn. Mrs. Hawker steadied her shaking hand and handed her a hot cup filled with chamomile tea. She then took a seat beside her and listened patiently as Naomi told her about her fiancée, her suspicions and that, against Samantha's advice, she had confronted Judas about Mariah and the rumors Samantha had heard. "Judas denied it all, of course. He said Sam's always gonna be jealous of me because niggas saw her as a downgrade. She should have held down her position instead of siding with a nigga that got knocked out the game. All this, he had the nerve to say when I told him he was bullshitting and to tell Mariah she was sacked," Naomi explained. "Firing Mariah is stupid, Naomi, and you know it. Did Samantha tell you that I was fucking anyone else?" Judas had asked flippantly as he sat in his boxers and vest top in the dark. He had been flicking through the channels on their digital TV, and every so often, he would check the time on his mobile or get up and peek through the blinds. "This isn't a joke, Judas. I'm firing Mariah and that's that. What do I look like paying a bitch to fuck my man?" Naomi sucked her teeth and asked. She put all the pieces of her suspicions in one bowl and baked the first conclusion that was reasonable enough to make sense. "I'm tired of you getting these tramps pregnant, Judas. I gave that bitch a job and you pity fuck her, put her up in our building and have the cheek to have my sister covering for your ass," she continued, looking at him in disgust, "I heard what you said to Sydney about not wanting the baby and I agree. We have a child on the way and if you deal with her situation now, we can bury this little episode and prepare for the arrival of our own." "How dare you tell me what to do with the life of my child?" Judas had exclaimed, leaping out his chair, getting up in Naomi's face. His clenched fists were a reaction from an old habit, one he'd promised Naomi he'd lose for the sake of their love. He pounded his fist into the nearest wall, startling Naomi, and caused her to jump in fright. He brushed past her, disgusted that such a proposal would escape her lips. She knew how Judas felt about the subject of a termination. It was an unforgivable deed, something that could never be undone.

Chapter 27

Shelly stood over Special in Sydney's bedroom, carefully pulling the straightening comb through her daughter's naturally thick, curly hair. "Why can't I just get my hair straightened like Auntie Syd does?" Special winced as the steam from the hot comb scorched her ear. "Because straightening costs money," Shelly answered, holding the tail comb between her teeth. "And it breaks your hair," Brittany looked up, winked then went back to flicking through an Essence magazine she'd found on Sydney's bedroom floor. It hadn't gone unnoticed that Special was becoming grown, Shelly still had a box full of colourful hair clips that Special had refused to wear now that she was in year nine. It was becoming harder and harder for Shelly to use the overprotective parent excuse to manipulate Special into staying home. It wasn't just fast girls that landed themselves in trouble, Shelly had been an A* student when Bradley had sexually abused her, impregnating her at thirteen. She wanted the best for daughter, yet she had failed in every department she tried. She couldn't even provide suitable accommodation for her baby, let alone keep her safe from the streets she so desperately wanted to wonder. "Hey, my money making bitches!" Sydney sang, looking flushed and weighed down with shopping bags at her bedroom door, "where's Naomi?" she asked as she shut the door, and rested her bags on the floor. "Judas let us in before he left out for his mum's. He said Naomi went to church," Brittany looked up from her magazine and replied. She remembered little about the night before but the stale taste in her mouth from the champagne she awoke with assured her she hadn't made it sober through the night. "I thought your sinning ass went with her," Shelly joked, kissing Sydney's cheek. She was unable to hug her with the heated comb in her hand. "Who, me? Please," Sydney laughed, "I've just come back from Westfield's. You know how I am when I got money to spend," she added, taking two white envelopes out of her Paul's Boutique handbag. She passed one to Brittany and threw the other to Shelly which happened to land in Special's lap. "What's this?" Shelly asked as she took her hands out of her daughter's hair and reached for the envelope to inspect its contents. "1, 2, 3, 4... It's five grand, Mums," Special said, emptying the neatly folded notes of twenties into her lap before Shelley could stop her. "You shouldn't even get yours," Sydney sneered at Brittany, "what were you thinking, drinking yourself under the table? Next time, and you're lucky there's gonna be a next time, don't fuck up! Shit almost fell to pieces because of that stunt you pulled." "I know and I'm sorry. It's just... This Craig thing, I still can't find him and its starting to fuck me up," Brittany admitted, "I passed by his parents house in Lake Side but his sister said she didn't know he'd moved and she had no idea where he was." "So?" Shelly asked, continuing with Special's hair. Special was busy folding the money back up and putting it back in the envelope. "So, I at least wanna know what the deal is between us! I can't accept that he would just fuck me over the way he has." "Your language," Shelly cleared her throat and pointed to her child. "Shit, sorry, Spech." Brittany replied and covered her mouth. Shelly shook her head and rolled her eyes. She would have given anything to have the opportunities that Brittany had been given in her life. She'd dated ball players, a doctor and a bachelor who owned several apartments in the city but Brittany tended never to think of the future, securing herself financially so she wouldn't have to depend solely on a man. "It's okay, Auntie Britt," Special snickered, "I know how you feel. That's why I won't date Samuel Claw until I gots my own," Special added, standing to look at her hair in mirror on the wardrobe door. "Well excuse me, Miss Special!" said Sydney, falling out on the bed in laughter, "you better not date this Samuel Claw until you're 25 and married with 3 babies or your mum's gonna hurt somebody." "Damn right I will," Shelly raised her left brow and replied. "Pleaseee, Auntie Syd. I don't even like Samuel, he's a bully. I like Kieran Clarke but I don't think he likes me like that," Special shyly cooed. "Ooo, Kieran Clarke. He sounds like a thug," Brittany teased, forgetting she was talking to a thirteen year old. "Kieran ain't a thug, Auntie Britt; he's a really nice guy. People might think he's trouble 'cause he bunks and stuff but he ain't. He's just sad," Special replied innocently. "Oh, okay. Why's he sad?" Brittany asked, putting her book down and entertaining her favorite, and only, unrelated niece. "'Cause his daddy's in jail," Special said flatly, "Kieran only speaks to his brother." "Yeah, well, that's too bad for Kieran. I don't want you going outta your way to cheer this young boy up," Shelly said as she was touching up her own hair. She watched from the corner of her eye as Sydney pulled her phone out of her purse, checked her messages and then put it down on the bed in a huff. "Baby, go into the kitchen and get yourself a drink," Shelly said to Special. Special was used to being sent out of the room when Shelly and her aunties were indulged in grown folks talk. "Okay," Special replied and bounced out the room. Special stood by the closed door just long enough to overhear Sydney mention her encounter with her ex boyfriend, Aaron, at last night's convention before she headed towards the lounge to use the phone. Special hadn't been able to stop thinking about Kieran and all the time they had spent together in the library after school. It was easy for people to perceive his harsh tone and non-responsive manner as him being bitter and stubborn but, deep down, he was genuinely sweet. Kieran had told Special that his father had been in prison for as long as he could remember and he didn't know how he was going to handle having a strange man waking up and sleeping in his home when he was to be released in the following year. "Good evening, Mrs. Clarke, this is Special. Please may I speak with Kieran?" Special asked nervously into the cordless phone. She'd last spoken to Kieran on Friday. He'd given her his number and told her to hit him up if she ever needed to talk. "Hold on a minute, honey," Kieran's mother politely responded. "Kieran!" Special heard Mrs.

Clarke call before Kieran came rushing to the phone. "What's up, Special?" Kieran picked up the receiver and asked without inquiring who was on the other end. This made Special blush. "Hey Kieran," Special said, sounding out his name. They'd become quite close during the last half term but for Special it was nowhere near close enough.

Chapter 28

Judas pulled a '03 hip-hop mix CD out of his car sound system, replaced it with Drake's 'Comeback Season' and turned the volume to its highest as he drove down Kingsland High Road towards Warwick Grove. Sunday lunch with his mother, his daughters and their mothers was an event he'd rather avoid but it was enough to keep the women off his back throughout the week. It also kept them singing his praises as a father who not only financed their lives but spent quality time with his girls. He laughed at the thought of Naomi joining his mother and the mothers of his five children around the table on a Sunday afternoon. He then parked his car in his mother's driveway and made his way to the house. greeting Keion, his daughter Brooklyn's mother, as she stood at the door in all her ghetto glory. "How's it hanging, superstar?" Keion asked, playfully grabbing Judas's manhood through his paints as he slipped past her through the door. "Where's Brooklyn?" he asked, removing Keion's hand from between his legs. "She's in the kitchen with Stitches and your mum," Keion replied, following behind Judas. Mrs. Mendez divorced Mr. Mendez long ago but refused to change her name from one she'd used for 31 years. She stood over a hot stove with a ladle in her hand, stirring a large pot of rice. "Hey, beautiful," Judas sang. He snuck up behind his mother and hugged her tight before planting a loving kiss on her cheek. "Judas, this is hot, let me finish up here, boy!" Mrs. Mendez blushed, acting as if she couldn't care less that her only son had just walked through her door. Five grand-daughters were enough to make Mrs. Mendez the proudest mother alive; she loved spending time with them. She'd take all of them to church with her on Sunday mornings and then bring them back to her house where she'd provide them with a meal she doubted any of them ever had at home. "Sup, Stitches?" Judas asked, sticking his finger in the bowl of icing sugar Stitches was busy mixing. "Judas," Stitches replied, greeting him only by name. She was still pretty pissed off by his reaction towards her proposal to him the other day. "Daaaddy!" Brooklyn and Tameerah sang in unison as they rushed their father to the floor. Shayanne and Ameerah both ran from the lounge to greet their father whilst Kayla, the oldest of the five, stood shyly by the door. "Okay, okay, let me up," Judas chuckled, tickling both of his daughters in an attempt to get free, "look at all these pretty girls I've got." Sheba, Tracey, and Victoria broke up their Maury debate, switched off the show they were watching in the lounge and bounced into the kitchen, following the sound of their daughters' giggles and yelps. They all stood watching, as did Mrs. Mendez, at the beauty of Judas and their girls. "Miss Kayla, Daddy ain't gonna get a hug?" Judas stood and asked his oldest daughter as she stood quietly by her mum. Whilst Victoria, Kayla's mother, was still hugely in love with Judas, Kayla didn't know much about the person that crept into her mother's bed some nights. "I got 10 boxes with my favorite girls' names on 'em but if Miss Kayla doesn't give Daddy a hug, ain't nobody getting one," Judas continued, stretching his arms out and whilst his daughters and their mothers excitedly urged Kayla to hug her dad. Kayla reluctantly fell into her father's arms and flashed him a fake smile when he squeezed her tight. She had long, dark, silky hair and skin that glowed almost like gold. Her green eyes sat in her head like emeralds while her lips were a natural rosy red, just like her mother's. Judas couldn't help but notice that Kayla was now wearing a bra and could only dread the day she wore a thong. "Okay, enough of the mushy stuff, I want my gift," said Keion, holding out her hand, causing laughter amongst the women in the kitchen. "I want mine too," Brooklyn screamed. "Me too, Daddy," the rest of the girls cried. "And there I was thinking you guys were making all that noise because you missed me. I'm hurt," Judas played, entertaining his daughters but directing his statement Keion's way. "Excuse me," Stitches said plainly, squeezing passed Judas to lay the table. She could feel Victoria and Sheba glaring at her from afar but she really couldn't have cared less. "Mummy, look at what Daddy bought us. It's a chain and it fits into a heart. Here, there's one for you and one for me," Tameerah said, bouncing around the table with her father's gift around her neck and her mother's gift in her hands. "Oh, that's beautiful, baby. Your daddy sure knows how to make a girl feel special," Stitches smiled sarcastically as she took the chain out her daughters' hand. The light-weighted chain and pendent was pretty but Judas had a cheek to produce such a pendant to the mothers of his children. The pendants together spelt 'Daddy's Little Girl' but apart one pendent said 'Daddy's' whilst the other said 'Little Girl.' "Daddy just wants to keep his girls happy," Judas shrugged, assisting his into their seats. Victoria, Sheba and Tracy sat next to their daughters around the table, Keion lingered for Judas to take his place and Stitches helped Mrs. Mendez with the food. "This looks good mum," said Judas, taking his place next to Brooklyn. Brooklyn was soon forced to give her seat to her mother and sat next to Sheba instead. Mrs. Mendez sat next to her youngest granddaughter, Tameerah, leaving an open seat next to Judas and herself. "You ladies out did yourself in the kitchen today," Judas complemented Stitches and his mum. They'd laid out a feast of fried chicken, string beans, fried yams, macaroni and cheese, rice and peas, steamed salmon, salad and bakes. "My babies need to eat right and grow strong and healthy like their father. I don't want them looking like these lean women out there who are talking about how they want to be a size zero, or six." "Well I'm a size 8, Mrs. M, and my baby has got some meat on her bones," Victoria said in-between bites of her meat. "I gots some meat, Grandma," Brooklyn giggled with a mouth full of food. "Yes you have, sugar," Mrs. Mendez smiled, "I sure know you can eat." "Maybe you should help out in the kitchen sometime, Keion. Show us some of those skills you got," said Stitches, neatly cutting her chicken and picking up a small piece with her fork. "Girl, she's tryna play you. She knows damn well you can't cook," Sheba whispered loudly in Keion's ear. "Well Brooklyn must be eating something good," Stitches replied, "I'm just saying, the kitchen is a place a mother should know her way around and looking at Brooklyn, Keion seems to know how to do her thing." Sheba shook her head slightly embarrassed. She and Keion were best friends way before Judas had them both blinged out and pregnant. Judas was just another 'thing' they shared. "You know what, Stitches, who asked you?" she clashed her cutlery down onto her plate and bent forward to speak up for herself, "everyone knows that the only reason you spend so much time in the damn kitchen with Mrs. M is because you know none of us out here can stand your stuck up ass." "Yeah, sure, Keion, I just love spending my Sunday afternoons in a hot ass kitchen, waiting hand and foot for your lazy ass," Stitches spat back before Mrs. Mendez cleared her throat loud enough for both women to realize their banter had become disrespectful, foul mouthed, and had disrupted the atmosphere around the table. "I don't know where you women get your energy to fuss all the time but wherever you find it, I suggest you leave it there before you bring my grand-babies to church. They don't need to be hearing all this noise; tell 'em, Judas," Mrs. M said, chewing on a piece of chicken bone. "She's right," Judas said with a full mouth, "you think just because they don't repeat what you women are saying that they don't take all your smart talk in?" "Well she started it," Keion retorted, picking up her folk and playing with her food. Keion had a habit of snarling at Stitches from afar. She'd pass comments about her to the other women but never to her face. It was typical that when Stitches thought it was appropriate to voice her mind, Mrs. Mendez and Judas would team up to call her out. "Mummy, I don't feel well," Tameerah moaned as she crossed her arms around her stomach and doubled over in pain. Stitches and Judas drew back their chairs and rushed to her side. "Maybe it was something she ate," Keion said snidely as Judas and Stitches removed Tameerah from the table. They brought Tameerah to the lounge where she curled up on the couch, sucking her thumb. "Ain't she too old to be doing that?" Judas asked Stitches who had begun packing Tameerah's bag. "It's a comfort thing, it doesn't bother me so it shouldn't bother you," Stitches replied bluntly. She refused to look at Judas. Instead, she stomped into the hallway to retrieve her daughter's shoes and coat along with her own. "Stitches!" Judas abruptly called after her. He followed her into the hallway, stopping her from returning to the lounge. "Get out my way, Judas. I'm taking Tameerah home," Tameerah demanded, shifting her weight to one side to stand her ground. "Let me drive you," Judas offered, stroking her face. He may have said some harsh things to her on the phone but the idea of her, or any of his daughter's mothers, with another man made his blood boil. "I drove my own damn car!" Stitches exclaimed, slapping Judas's hand away. "Well, let me at least tail you to make sure Tameerah settles down alright?" Judas pleaded. "Just get outta my way." Stitches then pushed him to the side and rolled her eyes. She'd given Judas all the chances in the world but the truth was that she knew he wasn't going to change. Judas picked up the shoe she'd dropped and let her pass. He then followed behind her into the lounge and stood helpless while she assisted their daughter with her coat. "Tash, can I say I'm sorry? And can we put all this in the past?" Judas asked as he picked up Tameerah when Stitches had finished buttoning up her coat. "Whatever!" Stitches replied, now buttoning up her own coat. She followed Judas into the kitchen and held her head high when she walked past Keion and Sheba to kiss Mrs. M goodbye. Keion looked like she was shitting in her jeans, watching Judas play the doting father to him and Stitches' child. "Put that baby to bed and give her something warm to drink," Mrs. Mendez instructed as Stitches respectfully kissed her on the cheek. Stitches and Judas left his mother's house and Judas then stuck to his word and tailed Stitches home. "You need to turn your tone down. I'm trying to settle Tameerah down to sleep," Stitches warned Judas, sticking her head around her daughter's bedroom door. He hadn't shown any concern for his daughter's health upon entering her flat. "You okay, baby?" she asked as she stroked her daughters face. Tameerah had fallen asleep in the back of her father's car but had stirred when her mother had warned Judas about his noise level. 'Why did I even let him follow me home?' Stitches wondered to herself. She pulled her mobile out of her pocket to see if she had any messages. She always put her phone on silent when she went to Judas' mother's house. She had 3 messages from Cee and another from a client who wanted to arrange a time to get the bandages changed on his wound. Two of Cee's messages were from Stitches' operator, letting her know she had missed his call. The other was a text message he'd sent not long ago saying he missed her and couldn't wait until the following weekend. Stitches smiled while she read Cee's message. She then opened Tameerah's bedroom door and stepped into the hallway where Judas' loud mouth led her into the kitchen. "And you think I wasn't?" she heard him say. "I'm telling you, Sticks, when Syd came in and put that duffle bag in my hand, I could have kissed her," he continued. Overhearing this made Stitches deter from interrupting Judas' call. Instead, she tip-toed back into Tameerah's room and listened from behind the door with intensity as Judas repeated to Sticks what Sydney had told him the night before. As usual, Judas had found a couple of young, dumb and desperate females to do his dirty work at his expense. "I can't lie, I was hesitant about sending the three of them in blind but Syd said her girl Brittany brought them through," Judas carried on. Stitches heard him pull out his chair and listened as he paced the kitchen. She couldn't hear Sticks at all. "I feel you, I feel you, Bruv, but I doubt one girl is gonna be brazen enough to intercept our team. You can watch her though; do some digging and see what comes up. Either way, I want my money from Cee. I know that motherfucker ain't wised up on me hitting him the first time and there's no way the second incident can be pinned on me," Judas continued while Stitches listened in despair. Her mind was doing overtime, frantically trying to make sense of the similar events the two men in her life had recently shared. "I'm the man around these parts and he owes me big. I don't care if his own mother robbed him or the devil himself. That thieving motherfucker is lucky my dad is making me spare his life." When those wicked words crawled out of Judas's mouth, Stitches couldn't help but gasp. She unintentionally leaned against Tameerah's bedroom door and accidently slammed it shut. She quickly moved from the door and bent down beside Tameerah, acting like she'd been comforting her while she slept. "Nah, I'm with Tash," Stitches heard Judas say before he abruptly opened Tameerah's bedroom door. He walked up behind Stitches, still on the phone, and gently ran his fingers through her hair.

PENAL CODE
Section 487(d)(1)
GRAND THEFT AUTO

Billie Dureyea Shell

THE SPOKESMAN

The Spokesman woke up on this beautiful morning not feeling any sympathy or the slightest regret for what he's about to handle. The work must be done. The only thing he had swimming in his mind. The work must be done. No matter the consequences. He got up from his king size bed and stretched. He walked over to the window and opened the curtains. What a wonderful day it is, he thought. Finally, I will get what's mine. He took a quick shower and sang love songs the entire time. He got out of the shower and continued to give himself the nicest shaven face you will ever see. Got to look good for the big day. He went into his closet and picked out his street gear. He put on a tee-shirt, jeans, Air Force 1's and an Atlanta fitted cap. He took one look in the mirror. Damn, I look good. He shut the closet door before going into the kitchen. He made himself a nice peanut butter and jelly sandwich. He sat at the dining room table and flipped through his contact list while he ate. "Here we go." He muttered with a mouth full. He removed a card and stared at it to make sure it was the correct one. Absolutely, it was the one. He read the words across the card to himself. "Private Investigator, Lenny Daverson." He hated Lenny with every ounce of blood he possessed in his body. But today, today he needed him. Today was the day he would love him. Today, if he paid close attention and did his job the way detectives are supposed to. Lenny would make him the happiest man in the entire world. He took the final bite of his sandwich and flipped the card into his pocket. No more delays, he must act now before he would miss this perfect opportunity. The work must be done. He grabbed his car keys and headed for the door. He locked up the house and got into his car. He sang along with Usher while he drove to the other side of town. Out of sight, out of mind. He thought about this situation numerous times before. This was definitely the best way to handle it. He found a busy gas station. Good mixed crowd. Nobody on this side of town would notice him. He parked his car at pump eight. He went inside and paid for some gas. He walked pass his vehicle without bothering to set the system up. He thought if someone was to notice him. They would approach him while he's standing at the car pumping gas or on the pay phone. His mind decided to handle that instantly. The pay phone was at the far end of the gas station. He walked over nonchalant, not wanting anybody to notice him. He retrieved the card from his pocket. He lifted the phone and dialed the private investigator's number. The phone rang three times and a woman answered. "Hold please." One minute later detective Lenny answered. "This is Inspector Daverson." The Spokesman smiled. "Let's get to the point. You're looking for Twenty, right?" Lenny felt his spine quiver. "Who is this?" "Does it matter? All you need to understand is that I know the time and place Twenty's next lift will be. Get your pen and pad."

Chapter 2

BLIND MAN

Twenty stepped out onto his room balcony. "Damn it feels good outside." Today is payday for him. Later tonight, he is going to lift the last car on the list for a buyer name, Money. The car is a 1969 Boss 302. Money, a notorious drug dealer on the other side of town who loves old school cars. He created a list of his fifteen most wanted cars and hired the best car thief around to handle the job. Each car was valued over $100,000. The job is for one million dollars and the man who is known to be the best, is Twenty. He has been lifting vehicles for anybody who had money since he was seventeen. This is the way he survives. He even has his own crew called, The Lifters. Three years of lifting vehicles professionally and this one is going to be his biggest payout. He has already received half the money up front and the other half he would get when the job is completed. His team of lifters included his best friend,

Jeff. He has known Jeff since the first grade. The second member of his team is Paula. They met Paula when they were thirteen years old. They lifted their first car in a grocery store parking lot. They saw a 96' Chevy Impala on 26-inch rims left running. They thought the car was beautiful and Twenty wanted it. It's funny how your best friend gets dragged into tough situations. Although, Jeff wasn't about to let Twenty steal the car all by himself. The coast was clear. At least, they thought the coast was clear. Twenty rushed over to the vehicle with Jeff close behind. Twenty hopped in the driver seat and Jeff hopped in the passenger's. Twenty put the car in drive and floored the pedal burning out of the parking lot. They got halfway down the block before hearing a voice in the back seat. It was Paula waking up from her nap. "What are you doing in my dad's car?" She asked sheepishly. Twenty was super excited about lifting his first car that he didn't notice the girl in the back seat. "What the hell!" He swerved the car because he was a little nervous that there was someone in the car with them. "A girl is in the back seat!" Jeff yelled hysterically. "What's going on?" Paula climbed over the front seat. "What are you doing little girl?" Twenty asked. He swerved the car back on track. "I'm twelve going on thirteen. In one month I'll be a teenager for your information. I'm not little." Paula answered with attitude.

"Twenty!" Jeff yelled. "We got to get out of this car for the police come. I don't want to go to jail man. I'm only thirteen." "Shut up you big baby." Paula hissed without knowing what was going on. "Why would the police come?" Twenty turned to her attention. Suddenly, he was struck by her beauty. This was the prettiest girl he has ever seen in his life. She had caramel skin, brown hair, and hazel eyes. He was lost for words while staring at her. How was he to answer? "Twenty!" Jeff yelled hysterically. Twenty focused back on the road. He had swerved into oncoming traffic. "Shit!" A car was coming right at them. He maneuvered the Chevy back into the proper lane. The Impala kept swerving out of control and they hit a fire hydrant. The boys got out and ran for it. Jeff took off first and Twenty was right behind him, but he stopped. He ran back to the car. "Hey… hey! You ok!" Paula didn't move. He pulled her from the car. She hit her head pretty good on the dashboard. Too late to run. The police showed. They took Twenty away and he got put on probation until he was eighteen. Paula would never forget what he did by coming back for her. The next time they had met was their tenth-grade year. Ever since she turned bad girl, she's been a part of The Lifters. Twenty loved her bravery. The last member of the team was a computer geek named Tony, but Twenty called him Tech. They met in computer class. Twenty noticed how good he was with solving problems with engines. Twenty came to him one day and flat out asked him did he want to be a part of the team. Tech being the smartest guy in school without any friends, agreed. From zero friends too three friends is how he looked at it. There were people who cared about him, real friends not computer friends, but real friends at school. Twenty used Tech to fix all the cars they had lifted. If something happened to one of the vehicles while they were on the move. Tech would fix the problem at the garage before the vehicle was delivered to the buyer. Tech was the best and he had the best friends. Twenty went back into the bedroom. He picked his phone up from the nightstand and dialed his best friend's number. Jeff answered in two rings. "Twenty," "Jeff," Twenty took the sheets off a fine exotic redbone. Twenty was addicted to the fast life. Money, cars, clothes, drinking, and his biggest addiction were women. He loved being with a different woman. That's why Paula never hooked up with him except for two times, one being prom night. Paula had turned down every boy at school except for Twenty. He took her that night and they had the best time. Paula knew he was a player and she gave him some anyway. That was her first time. After prom, they decided to go back to their ways. Their friendship was more important. The other time happened two months ago when Paula had her twentieth birthday. They had got drunk and ended up in bed together. Another slip. It felt more like love to Paula, but decided against it. She knew better than that so she bottled it up and kept it to herself. "What's going on man? You ready to get this money?" "You know it," Jeff replied. "Are you?" The girl woke from the chill of not having any covers over her naked body. She looked at Twenty puzzled. Twenty tossed her clothes at her. "Time for you to leave." He pointed to the door coolly. She frantically grabbed her clothes cursing him out the entire time she put them on. She slammed the door with great force as she left that it shook every picture on the wall. "Whoa, crazy." He muttered. Jeff knew exactly what was taking place. He knew about Twenty being the player he was. He was doing the usual, putting another one out after a long night of hot sex. "Redbone from the club last night? "Yeah man, I didn't know she was going to be that damn emotional. I just met her and she knows she doesn't live here." Twenty joked while sitting on the edge of the bed and falling back. Jeff laughed through the phone. "Well, maybe she thought she did. You need to start being more careful." "Why is that?" "These women are crazy. Once they met the guy they really want to be with. He uses her and then she goes five years without dating. Finally, she meets a guy like you all tattooed up, nice teeth and muscles, 6'3, 220lbs, cornrows and great conversation. She figures in her mind, she's met the right guy. Soon as you dump her like trash the next night. All hell breaks loose. Now she's trying to kill you and every corner you turn man. She's there.""Damn," Twenty said. "You described me well. Have we dated?" He joked. Jeff laughed. "You think that shit is funny but I'm telling you man. Watch out. Females are emotional creatures, my man." "Thanks for being my counselor of love. I can handle myself, buddy. I've been doing it for twenty years now. I pretty much got a good grip. Anyway," he got up. He was pissed because he was comfortable. "You talk to Tech?" "He said he'll be at the garage waiting for us." "What about Paula?" Twenty asked. "With this being the last car. I didn't think you wanted me to tell her. The three of us don't need to lift one car, do we?" Twenty thought about that. Hell, he's right. The three of us don't need to lift one car. Really, it would only take the two of them to do it. Jeff would drop him off at the Antique Cars of Atlanta tonight. He would lift a 69' Boss 302 with no problem. The older cars were always the easiest cars to lift. He would race the car back to the garage. Tech would look it over. First thing in the morning Money would be there to pick up the fifteen cars Twenty had stored for him. Pay him the $500,000 owed and it would be simple as that. A piece of cake. Paula could pick her portion up tomorrow when the money arrives. Her job was finished until the next order. "You're right about that. Meet me at the garage so we can go over the final plan and inspect all of the cars again. Tomorrow's the day and we don't need any problems." "Cool, give me an hour and I'll be there." "See ya,"Twenty hung up the phone. Out of this deal, he was making $400,000. Everyone else was making $200,000 for the job. That's good money with a team of four. Twenty entered the garage and greeted Tech. He was already inspecting the cars. Jeff came ten minutes later. They spent the rest of the afternoon going over the plan. It started to get late and Antique Cars of Atlanta closed two hours ago. Jeff drove Twenty to the dealer. Twenty saw the beautiful Boss 302 through the glass of the building. "Look at it. That's money right there." "Twenty, man I don't know." Jeff was hesitant. "I got a bad feeling about this one." "Jeff every car we lifted, you had a bad feeling." Twenty got out and shut the door. "Stop worrying. This is the last one and we get paid. We'll chill for a while after this, cool?" "Cool." He gave Twenty some dap. "Be safe, bruh." "No doubt," Twenty vanished into the night.

Chapter 3

THE CHASE

Twenty crept along the building of Antique Cars of Atlanta. He surveyed his surroundings carefully. When he was certain no security was in proximity of him. He made his move further around the building while staying close to the wall. He came to the back door. He retrieved his lock pick tool from his pocket. "Piece of cake." He muttered to himself. The back door wouldn't be any challenge to him. He picked harder doors before. He stuck the lock picking tool in the keyhole and listened carefully as he turned to pick it. He listened for all the correct clicks. He mastered the lock and on the last turn the door popped like magic. "Yeah baby, that's it." He muttered. Before he walked in he did what he normally does before walking through a door without knowing who's on the other side. Maybe security, maybe not. He didn't think security would be lurking around inside of a dark building waiting for him to come but what the hell. Better safe than sorry. He knocked on the door three solid times and ducked off. He patiently waited. Nobody was home. After two minutes he crept back to the door and opened it quietly as possible. He peeked his head in. Look at all these sweet cars just waiting for me to pick one, he thought. He crept in. "Anybody home. I just wanna borrow some sugar or a 69' Boss 302." He joked to himself. He cautiously searched for the area that would have the alarm pad. Tech told him he would have two minutes to disarm it after stepping foot in the building. If he didn't want the police all over his ass, he better get to it. He kept a cool demeanor as he scanned the room. "There we go, baby." He found the alarm pad on the center wall under an oil painting of an old Ford GT500. One minute to go. He hurried over. He flipped the alarm case down, revealing the number pad. "Ok Tech, you fucking better be right or I'm fucked. What were the numbers, 3, 4, 0, 2?" He knew if he got the numbers wrong he would have one more chance. One more chance was something he wanted to avoid altogether. Tech told him if he got the code wrong the first time the pad would beep. Signaling to him he was wrong. The second time it would turn red and the police would be on him before he had the chance to whip his ass. What he needs is for the numbers to light up green, signaling that the alarm was disarmed.

Tech broke into the dealer's computer system and retrieved the code. That's how they were successful at entering dealerships that had cars on the list. Tech is a genius. Without him, it would be a brick through the window and a swift wiring of the vehicle then a fast getaway or prison. He was grateful to have Tech on the team. It gave him more leverage and with the extra needed time. There was no need to wire the vehicles anymore. He'll just find the keys instead. He punched the numbers on the pad. "3, 4, 0, 2." He mumbled pressing each button. The pad made a loud beep. "Fuck." He muttered. One more chance. Get it right or break for it, he thought. "Ok," he raised his hand, thinking about the code Tech told him over and over. "3, 4, 0, 3." He almost broke a sweat. Thinking he was going to have to break for it. The pad turned green after a long second. "Hell yeah." He found the key room without any problem. He found the mini safe with the key to the Boss. He began to pick it. The safe was already unlocked. "Dayum, somebody is going to get fired." He thought it was odd but brushed it off. Time is money. He hurried to the garage to lift it so he could drive the Boss out without any damages. Suddenly, the dealer's lights cut on. He heard freeze! "Fuck!" He rushed to the Boss and hopped in and fired up the engine. Police swarmed the car lot. "Get out of the car!" Daverson yelled. "Twenty!

It's over! Police are everywhere, you're cornered!"Twenty began to realize he was set up. They were waiting for him. What to do? He looked at the glass doors. "I can't go to prison." He floored the Boss and busted through the glass doors. The engine growling through the parking lot. He shifted the motor into high gear. "Fuck!" The police were at the front entrance. He shifted to reverse and burnt out backward, leaving a trail of smoke. He couldn't get far. A helicopter lowered close enough to the ground and blocked the car in. The police had weapons ready for business. He watched his young life go. No choice, he surrendered.

ABOUT THE AUTHOR

New York Times & International Best Selling Author Billie Dureyea Shell was born in Compton California and now lives in Ladera Heights with his wife and kids who he loves to spend time with.

He is the Owner of several properties in the Los Angeles area and gives back to his community by providing low income housing to those who need it.

He stated "It doesn't matter where you at or where you from it's what you do with your time. There's nothing you can't do if you put your mind to it".